"I know you, Amy. You'll never go all the way."

Maybe she wouldn't if she didn't want a baby with him so very much. "I will, too!"

"Then prove it." Teddy turned to her, making no effort to hide his desire. "Go into the bedroom. Take off your clothes. And wait for me."

She turned on her heel and stormed out of the room. "I thought it was going to be a lot easier married to you!"

"No kidding!"

Huffing in exasperation, she marched over to the bed. Stood staring down at it for one long second.

"This is to make a baby," she whispered to herself, already toeing off her boots. "Our baby. And he or she will be made in the spirit of tenderness and hope and love."

This baby would be the ultimate Christmas gift to each other....

Dear Reader,

My husband is also my best friend. We became great pals as we fell in love. But what if, I wondered, that hadn't been the case? What if we had been buddies first and then realized we wanted to date? Would our romance have developed in the same way?

Thirty-five-year-old Teddy McCabe and Amy Carrigan have been friends since elementary school. Wary of risking their friendship, they have never allowed themselves to think of each other as anything but companions, although they have joked about having kids together one day. As the Christmas season begins, and Amy's thirty-second birthday approaches, they realize they might never get the family they both want so much if they don't start down another less traditional path.

So they rush off to the justice of the peace, determined to get it done, and move on to Phase Two of operation baby-making. They already know each other. They're not planning to have sex. This is going to be a piece of cake! They don't bargain on the complications that quickly—and inevitably—ensue.

But as anyone who has ever said "I do" knows… marriage changes everything!

I hope you have as much fun reading this holiday story as I did creating it.

Best wishes to you and all your loved ones,

Cathy Gillen Thacker
THE RANCHER'S CHRISTMAS BABY

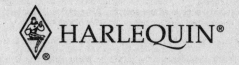

TORONTO • NEW YORK • LONDON
AMSTERDAM • PARIS • SYDNEY • HAMBURG
STOCKHOLM • ATHENS • TOKYO • MILAN • MADRID
PRAGUE • WARSAW • BUDAPEST • AUCKLAND

ISBN-13: 978-0-373-75193-8
ISBN-10:   0-373-75193-1

THE RANCHER'S CHRISTMAS BABY

www.eHarlequin.com

Printed in U.S.A.

ABOUT THE AUTHOR

Cathy Gillen Thacker married her high school sweetheart and hasn't had a dull moment since. Why? you ask. Well, there were three kids, various pets, any number of automobiles, several moves across the country, his and her careers and sundry other experiences (some of which were exciting and some of which weren't). But mostly, there was love and friendship and laughter, and lots of experiences she wouldn't trade for the world. Please visit her Web site at www.cathygillenthacker.com.

Books by Cathy Gillen Thacker

HARLEQUIN AMERICAN ROMANCE

Chapter One

"I had no idea it was this bad." Amy Carrigan reached over and took the hand of her best friend, Teddy McCabe, the day after Thanksgiving.

He squeezed her hand reassuringly. "Same here." Being careful to keep to the other side of the yellow tape surrounding the century-old community chapel in downtown Laramie, Texas, Teddy let go of her hand and walked around, surveying what remained of the previously beautiful church.

The once towering live oak tree that had been struck by lightning at the advent of the previous night's thunderstorm had a jagged black streak down what remained of the trunk. The rest of the tree had taken out the bell tower and fallen through the center of the church roof.

By the time the fire department had arrived, the white stone chapel was engulfed in flames. Nearly half the wooden pews had been destroyed. And though the exquisite stained-glass windows were amazingly still intact, the walls were covered with black soot, the velvet carpeting at the altar beyond repair.

Fortunately, no one had been hurt, and plans were already being made to restore the town-owned landmark.

"Do you think they're really going to be able to get this restored in three weeks' time?" Amy asked.

"Given the number of volunteers that have already signed up to help with the cleanup, yes," Teddy replied.

"Trevor and Rebecca were supposed to have the twins' christening here on the twenty-third."

"We'll get it done," Teddy promised.

Amy hoped so. Although there were numerous other churches in the area, the community chapel was where everyone got married and had their children christened. It was small and intimate and imbued with tradition and hope.

Amy had dreamed of being married here.

Teddy studied her. "Everything okay?"

"What do you mean?"

"You've seemed blue. You hardly cracked a smile during the Thanksgiving festivities yesterday."

Amy had been hoping no one would notice.

She walked around to survey the damaged landscaping around the chapel. "I had a headache."

Teddy ambled along behind her. He had a good nine inches on her. And though they *both* owned ranches and worked outdoors—she growing plants, Teddy breeding horses—one might have a hard time discerning how physically fit she was because she was so delicately boned and slender.

However, it came as no surprise to anyone that Teddy had ranching in his blood. After all, he had the broad shoulders and strong, rugged build of the McCabe men. Being around him like this always made her feel impossibly feminine…and protected.

"Headache or heartache?" Teddy probed.

Amy returned wryly, "Thank you, Dr. Phil. But I really don't need your psychoanalysis."

"That, my friend, is debatable." Teddy placed both hands on her shoulders and turned her so she had no choice but to look at him. "Come on, Amy." His grip tightened ever so slightly, the warmth of his palms transmitting through the fleece vest she wore. "Tell me what's going on."

Her skin tingling from the unexpected contact, Amy knelt to examine a fire-singed Buford holly bush. "It's nothing."

Teddy gazed at her compassionately. "Is it the birthday you have coming up in January?"

Amy glared at Teddy and stepped away. "Way to cheer me up, cowboy."

He exhaled. "Thirty-two is not old." He could say that because he was almost thirty-five.

Amy headed toward the parking lot located behind the chapel, where her pickup truck was parked. "It's not young, either."

"You have a lot to feel good about. A family who loves you and a lot of friends. Not to mention the best plant-and-tree nursery in the area."

Amy did feel proud. Over the last ten years, she had grown her business from a rented greenhouse to a prosperous concern.

"True, you don't have a house yet…." Teddy conceded with a frown.

Not like the one he had on his Silverado Ranch, anyway. "Now you're dissing where I live?"

The lines on either side of Teddy's mouth deepened. With the familiarity of someone who had been her friend since elementary school, he said, "You don't have to live in a tiny little trailer."

Amy shrugged off his concern. "It suits me just fine right

now. Besides, I want to pour all my money into expanding."

Laurel Valley Ranch currently comprised fifty acres and ten greenhouses. She grew everything from Christmas trees to perennials and starter plants, and even had a husband-and-wife team working for her full-time now.

"Then if it's not that…is it the time of year that's getting you down? The holidays…"

Not surprised that Teddy had seen through her defenses, Amy blurted out, "Can you really blame me?" Tears blurred her eyes. "Everywhere I look, everywhere I go, I'm reminded that Christmas is for kids—and I don't have any! And at the rate I'm going I might never have any!"

To her surprise, Teddy looked as if he were feeling the same. "Then, maybe," he said slowly, "it's time you and I both revisited the promise we made to each other."

Amy backed up until her spine touched the back of her pickup. "I was twelve and you were fifteen!"

Teddy propped a shoulder against the door, blocking her way into the driver side. "It doesn't mean it wasn't a good idea."

Amy stared at him, wishing she could say she was shocked by what he was proposing. The same crazy, irrational thought had been in the back of her mind for months now. She'd just been too romantic at heart to bring it up.

She took a deep breath and repeated the vow they had made. "You want us to marry and have babies together—as friends? Not two people who are wildly in love with each other."

Teddy exuded McCabe determination. "We said then if we didn't find anyone else to start a family with by the time we were thirty, that's what we would do. And let's face it," he continued ruefully, "we passed that mark a while ago."

Amy's heartbeat kicked up a notch and she put her hands on the metal door panel on either side of her, steadying herself.

"It's not like we haven't been looking for a mate or been engaged," Teddy argued. "We have. It didn't work out for either of us."

Teddy's march to the altar had been abruptly cut short two years ago. Amy hadn't fared any better herself; her engagement had ended in a firestorm of embarrassment and humiliation, five years prior.

Teddy took both her hands in his and looked down at her with a gentle expression. "I'm tired of waiting, Amy. Tired of wishing for that special someone to show up and change my life. Especially now that Rebecca and Trevor have had twins. And Susie and Tyler are expecting their first child."

Amy tightened her fingers in his. "It seems everyone we know is getting married, settling down." Her two older sisters, his two triplet-brothers…their friends and former schoolmates…

He held her gaze deliberately, his hazel eyes reflecting the disappointment he felt about the turn life had taken. "Except us."

Silence fell between them as a church bell began to ring in the distance.

The Christmas spirit that had been absent in her soul took root again.

"So what do you say?" Teddy took Amy's chin in his hand and a coaxing smile tugged at the corners of his lips. "How about we make this a Christmas we will always remember?"

"YOU DID WHAT?" LUKE CARRIGAN choked on his drink, later the same day.

Teddy had been fairly certain the overprotective older man would not readily accept anything but a traditional romance for his youngest daughter. In fact, Luke had been ready to start matchmaking to speed things along—if that was what it took to get Amy the husband and kids she deserved....

"Amy and I got married. This afternoon," Teddy repeated. They had driven to a justice of the peace in a neighboring county and cemented their deal before either of them could change their minds.

Teddy had no regrets.

He was sure this was the right thing, for both him and Amy. He only wished their families shared the sentiment. It appeared, as all four parents stared at them in shocked silence, that they did not.

Beside him, in a cranberry-red dress and heels that made the most of a slender frame and feminine curves, her pale-blond chin-length hair in tousled disarray, Amy looked even more beautiful than she had at the courthouse where the ceremony had taken place.

"Is this a joke?" Amy's mother, Meg Carrigan, finally managed to say.

Her sable-brown eyes widening as if to say *I told you this was going to be rough,* Amy moved closer to Teddy.

Sensing she needed a show of physical—as well as emotional—support, he wrapped his arm around her shoulders in a husbandly gesture that felt as new and un-familiar to him as the vows they had just taken.

Glad they had opted to break the news to their folks with a champagne toast in one of the private party rooms at the Wagon Wheel restaurant in Laramie, Teddy faced Amy's parents.

Luke was a family physician, Meg a registered nurse. They were used to dealing with highly emotional situations.

His parents were no lightweights, either.

Travis ran a cattle ranch, while his mother had founded the Annie's Homemade Food business.

Yet all four looked as if they could be blown over by the slightest wind.

"Of course it's not a joke, Mom," Amy retorted stiffly, as she stepped forward and passed the canapés around.

Annie McCabe struggled to understand. "You're not…" Teddy's mother paused and bit her lip as if not sure how to word it. She tried again, ever so gently this time. "Are you two expecting?"

Teddy swore beneath his breath, immediately earning the glares of both fathers.

"Sorry." Teddy poured more champagne for everyone. "And, no, to answer your question," he said tersely, feeling his patience waning, "of course we're not getting married because we have to!" Their parents were behaving as if he and Amy were two reckless teens, instead of competent, responsible adults.

"We don't have that kind of relationship!" Amy insisted.

"Then why did you get married?" Luke Carrigan countered, passing on the picadillo dip.

"Because we *want* to have a family." Teddy helped himself to the hearty nacho-style appetizer. "And we've decided to have one together."

This, at least, Teddy noted, was no surprise to either set of parents.

He and Amy had told everyone about their "promise to each other" when they were kids, to the point it had been joked about between the two families ever since.

Amy followed his lead, behaving as if she had absolutely no trepidation about confronting their families with their decision—when he knew darn well she had dreaded this contretemps as much as he had.

Looking beautiful and relaxed, she put several chili-flavored shrimp on a small plate. "We're just basing our marriage on friendship, instead of romantic love," she continued casually.

"Although we do love each other as friends," Teddy interjected.

Disappointment resonated all around.

Amy sent their parents a guilt-inducing look as she sipped on more champagne. "We had hoped y'all would support us in this."

"I don't see how we can," Meg Carrigan replied, gentle and direct as ever.

"Romantic love is the foundation of every successful marriage," Annie McCabe pointed out.

"And friendship," Amy argued, taking her place next to Teddy once again.

He slid an arm around her waist and brought her in close to his side. Unaccustomed to touching her this way, he was surprised at how warm and supple she felt.

What stunned him even more was the prompt reaction of his pulse.

Teddy breathed in slowly, trying to suppress his desire. Once he regained his equilibrium, he continued to regard their families with the take-charge attitude that was deeply ingrained in all the McCabes.

"We wanted y'all to be the first to congratulate us,"

Teddy said, unable to help but appreciate the soft lilac fragrance that clung to Amy's hair and skin.

Or in other words, he thought silently, letting his direct gaze speak the rest for him, *we're not here to ask your permission.*

To his relief, their parents seemed to get what he had not said out loud, for politeness' sake.

"And we wanted to prepare you for the likelihood of becoming grandparents very soon," Amy said.

Annie McCabe began to warm to the notion, despite herself.

Teddy smiled—he had known they would come around. Although, he had expected it would take a lot more time than this!

"Are you going to adopt?" his mother asked, hope shining in her soft eyes.

Teddy stiffened. This was the part about his arrangement with Amy he liked least. Although he understood why Amy had stipulated they do it this way, his healthy male ego couldn't help but be a bit bruised by this unconventional arrangement.

"No. We're having our children the new-fashioned way," Amy declared, her cheeks turning a delectable shade of pink.

"Via artificial insemination," Teddy finished for her.

Travis McCabe's brow furrowed. He stared at Amy as if unable to believe what he had just heard.

Teddy understood that, too. His parents had a deeply loving and passionate relationship that seemed to transcend all others. It was no wonder that they were thrown for a loop by this shocking news.

They were—like Amy's parents and his and Amy's newly married siblings—the lucky ones. Couples who seemed to have found it all.

Sadly, for him and Amy, that hadn't happened.

So although Teddy and Amy both still lamented the lack of perfection in their personal lives, they had decided that they'd rather not go through the rest of their lives alone.

Even if it meant making a few hard sacrifices.

"And that's okay with you?" Travis asked Teddy. "Having a baby through a *medical procedure?*"

Teddy shrugged.

"It works for the horses I've been breeding. They all seem happy enough. And as long as Amy and I get what we want in the end—kids—who really cares?"

Amy flashed Teddy a grateful smile.

Unfortunately, she was the only other person beside himself, Teddy noted, who looked accepting of the situation.

"Not to put too blunt a point on it," Dr. Carrigan refuted, his expression as grim and disapproving as Teddy's own father, "but what about your own sex drives?"

Amy's fair skin flushed an even deeper pink.

Teddy's heart went out to her. Embarrassing as this was for him, it had to be harder for a diehard romantic like Amy. He knew she had dreamed of finding her Prince Charming and having that fairy-tale wedding in the community chapel since she was a little girl.

Unfortunately, just when she thought her fantasies were finally coming true and she'd given her heart and soul to Ken Donoho, Amy had been forced to abruptly end her engagement.

Her reasons were never revealed to anyone outside her family and she had never wanted to talk about it since.

Teddy hadn't pushed her.

Friends did not do that to each other.

He had regretted, however, the damage the failed relationship had done to Amy's outlook on life.

She no longer trusted romance. No longer yearned for the kind of physical passion that would last a lifetime. She was looking for Security Man now.

And he understood that, better than anyone. After all, his own engagement had also ended abruptly—and painfully. The experience had left him equally mistrusting of the initial "infatuation" stage of a relationship.

Since he had been interested in the long haul—and a woman who was as entrenched in "reality" as *he*—Teddy hoped he and Amy had at last found what they had been looking for all along. The kind of deep abiding friendship and lifelong commitment that they could use as the foundation for the family they both wanted so badly.

To his disappointment, it looked to Teddy like all their parents could focus on was the lack of intimacy in his and Amy's union.

"So are the two of you *ever* planning to consummate your marriage?" Travis McCabe asked warily.

Eventually, Teddy thought. When the time was right.

To his surprise, Amy had other ideas. "We don't know…um…if that will ever happen." Amy looked as if she wanted to sink through the floor as she threw her hands up in dismay. "I mean, I know the rest of our lives seems like a long time. But we've promised each other no pressure in that regard, and we're both okay with it either way."

Teddy's parents shook their heads, as if they had both somehow landed in a warped fairy tale.

"What about in the meantime? Are you two even going to be living together?" Dr. Carrigan asked, looking at them both as if they had completely lost their minds. An emotion the other three parents also seemed to feel.

"Yes. Of course," Amy huffed.

"Absolutely," Teddy concurred.

"Where?" Meg Carrigan inquired. She moved in close to her husband, her brows knit with worry.

"At my place!" Amy and Teddy said in unison.

Luke Carrigan wrapped a supportive arm about his wife's waist as she narrowed her gaze at the flustered duo.

"Obviously, that remains to be worked out," Teddy said, grimacing.

"What happens if this marriage doesn't pan out?" Annie McCabe asked. She stepped closer to her husband, too. Her hand instinctively curled into Travis's.

Watching the two older couples lean on each other, the way they always had, made Teddy think, *That's the way marriage should be.*

Suddenly, he wondered if he and Amy would ever have that special connection. More important, was friendship going to be enough to sustain them?

Or would having a family—and their mutual affection—transform their platonic union into a real marriage?

Clearly, their parents did not think so.

But just because they had reservations did not mean it couldn't happen, Teddy rationalized.

Furthermore, it wasn't as if he and Amy hadn't tried to find happiness the traditional way.

The problem was, romance just hadn't worked for either of them. And probably, given their temperaments and expectations, never would.

Hence, they were obtaining a family for themselves the only way they could.

Beside him, Amy clearly agreed. "Teddy and I've already stipulated that should either of us decide it's a mistake and want out—and for the record, neither of us expect that will happen—then we'll get an annulment."

"As long as we don't consummate the marriage, it should be no problem," Teddy agreed.

"It will be a problem if there is a child involved when you two decide this," Travis McCabe countered.

Teddy knew how seriously every parent in the room took their responsibility toward their children. Luckily, he and Amy felt the same way.

Teddy took Amy's hand in his, and held it in much the same way his father was holding his mother's hand. "If we do want to end the marriage and we have a child—or children—by then, we've agreed on split custody. Since we both own businesses here in Laramie, and plan to reside here permanently, that should be an easy-enough thing to arrange. Not," Teddy added, before anyone could interrupt, "that either Amy or I expect it to come to that."

Amy's chin took on the familiar, defiant tilt. "Teddy and I've been friends forever and we're plenty old enough to know exactly what we're getting into."

"That," her father remarked grimly, "is debatable."

An hour later as Amy and Teddy walked out to his pickup truck, she said, "Well, it's official. Both our parents think we've made a huge mistake."

Teddy started to head for his own side of the vehicle, then stopped and cut across to Amy's side.

Ignoring her look of surprise—because this was the kind of thing he did for his girlfriends, not his casual female friends—he opened the passenger door for her.

As his wife, she deserved a lot more from him on every level. Starting now, Teddy decided, she would get it. As well as reassurance when she needed it—which she clearly did.

"Look, Amy. We know we're doing the right thing." He gazed at her tenderly, smiling until her face lit up and she smiled back. "We're going to be great parents. Giving each other a baby is the best Christmas present either of us could ever have."

Hope flared in her eyes, along with the confusion.

Seeing she still needed a little convincing, he gave her a playful tap on the nose. "Trust me on this," he told her softly. "Once you're pregnant, once we're one step closer to our dream, everyone else will be rooting for us, too."

Chapter Two

As they drove back to the Laurel Valley Ranch, Amy couldn't help but notice how good Teddy looked in the black Ultrasuede jacket and discreetly patterned tie, or how the dark olive hue of his dress shirt brought out the green of his eyes.

Whether gussied up—like now—or dirtied up from ranch work, Teddy McCabe was one fine specimen of a man. Add to that his amazing intellect and kind, compassionate nature and Amy knew she had chosen a fine husband for herself and father to her future children.

Now, if only everyone else could see that, too...

"So how do you want to do this?" Teddy asked, parking in front of Amy's trailer.

One wrist resting atop the steering wheel, he turned toward her. "You want me to wait around while you get your stuff? Or just go on ahead and wait for you at my house?"

Amy blinked at him in surprise, stunned by his matter-of-fact tone. "What are you talking about?"

Teddy flashed a smile and came around to get her door. "Well, obviously, now that we're married, we have to sleep somewhere—and I figured since I have horses to care for, that we'd be bunking at my place."

"For tonight," Amy acceded, accepting his help exiting the cab.

It was his turn to look surprised. "For every night," he specified, as if wondering why there was even a question. In his mind, it was already decided.

Her heels sank into the gravel drive, making walking difficult. Unease swept through her. She thought about something she'd heard.

People change when they get married.

Until now, she'd figured that was just the frustration talking, when the couple in question didn't really know each other—or hadn't allowed themselves to see the real character of the person they were marrying—until after the romance surrounding the wedding ceremony had faded, and reality sunk in.

She could not believe this was going to be the case for her and Teddy, since they had known each other for years and years—without the veil of romance.

She looked over at him and promptly stumbled. "Teddy, I'm not giving up my place."

He slid a hand beneath her elbow, to steady her. "I didn't ask you to do that."

Her spike heels did little better in the grass, and she lurched into him again. "You're asking me to move in with you."

Teddy frowned and wrapped an arm around her waist, pulling her in close to his side. "Because it makes sense," he said.

She scowled back and used her elbow to wedge more distance. "To you, maybe," she argued, pulse pounding.

"Come on, Amy." He paused as they reached the stoop leading up to her front door, his usual accommodating nature fading. "I admit I've only been in your trailer once or twice, and then only for a minute or two, but the ceiling is so low I can barely stand up straight."

He had a point there. Her travel-trailer home had not been made for a six-foot-four male with broad shoulders. He was unlikely to fit in her double bed and would likely hang over the edge of her sofa, too.

In fact, the six-hundred-square-foot space was so tiny she never did any entertaining there.

Not that she and Teddy had ever spent much time at either's place. Hanging out that way would have felt too much like dating. Instead, they'd preferred to go places together in town. The more casual the better—to avoid any intimate male-female interaction.

Which was what made it so awkward now. "Teddy, I—" Amy broke off as the couple who worked for her approached.

Both were in their midtwenties. A petite brunette, Sheryl Cooper was nearly eight months pregnant. Her husband, Ed, wasn't much taller than she and had gone prematurely bald.

Even before they'd learned they were expecting, they had been the picture of married bliss. Now, with their firstborn son on the way, they were over the moon.

Or at least they had been, Amy noted, taking in their tense, worried expressions. "What's wrong?" she demanded at once.

"We've been working in the greenhouses all afternoon and I started having contractions half an hour ago," Sheryl said, hand to her tummy. Her face was blotchy and dotted with perspiration. "I've had three now—all precisely ten minutes apart. It feels like I'm going into labor."

And they all knew it was too early for that to be happening.

"I've already called her obstetrician. I'm taking her over to the emergency room to get checked out." Ed looked as worried as Sheryl sounded.

"Anything I can do?" Amy asked in concern.

Ed shook his head and assisted Sheryl into the cab of their station wagon. "I'll let you know what the doc says." He climbed behind the wheel and drove off.

"I hope she's okay," Teddy said.

Amy released the breath she had been holding. She touched a hand to her throat. "Me, too."

He followed her inside. "So back to our plans for the evening…"

Amy looked around the frilly interior of her home. The overstuffed floral sofa, and pink, green, and white color scheme were perfect for her romantic nature. However, they did not suit a macho guy like Teddy at all.

Already, as he moved past the leather-bound trunk that served as her coffee table, past the banquette to the galley kitchen—which had a half-size everything—he looked cramped. Worse, he was making her feel crowded. Even a little breathless. So much so, she suddenly needed some time to herself.

Amy slipped off her wool dress coat and strode past the tiny bathroom to her bedroom.

She had to slip off her heels and climb over the double bed—which took up the entire space—to get to the closet to put her coat and shoes away. "Why do we have to spend the night together?" As she backed up on her knees, she caught him looking at her legs.

To her chagrin, he didn't so much as flush.

Instead, he lounged in the portal, arms crossed in front of him, as if he owned the place. "Is that a serious question?"

What had gotten into him?

"Obviously," Amy said stiffly, "it is."

Deciding she needed to get out of the cranberry silk-chiffon wrap-dress she'd gotten married in, Amy grabbed a pair of jeans and a pine-green chenille turtleneck sweater.

Teddy sighed with frustration.

Feeling equally frustrated, Amy slipped past him, into the bath.

Very much aware how different this evening would be if they were having a real wedding night—the over-the-top-romantic kind she had dreamed about her entire adult life—she stripped off her dress and peeled off her panty hose.

"We're married, Amy," Teddy reminded her through the closed door. He was beginning to sound impatient.

Amy walked back out with an arch look. "As friends only."

Maddeningly, Teddy stayed right where he was, giving her little room to maneuver in the cramped space. "It's still expected that we will reside together."

Refusing to admit he was quite clearly making his point—her trailer was too tiny for the both of them—she qualified right back, "Once I'm pregnant. But there's no rush for us to be together under the same roof until then."

Teddy rubbed the flat of his hand underneath his jaw and regarded her the same way he looked at one of his horses when the animal wasn't doing what he wanted it to do.

Amy knew that in those situations, Teddy always figured out how to get his way.

It was a quality all good leaders possessed—the ability to figure out how to get someone else to follow.

The problem was, she did not want him to be the leader in their marriage. She did not want either of them to be in a position to boss the other around. She wanted them to continue to do their own thing, in their own way, in their own time.

"So there is no reason we have to reside under the same roof tonight or any other night right now," Amy concluded.

"I think our parents would beg to differ on that point," he said dryly.

Normally, Amy liked to exchange ideas and witty remarks with Teddy. But not today. Not after the grilling they had just been through. What she wanted now was some peace and quiet. Privacy. Time to figure out how they were going to proceed with this hasty marriage of theirs.

Her bare feet planted firmly on the carpet, Amy told Teddy, "We've already established I don't care what they think."

"Then what," Teddy asked, advancing on her ever so slowly, his low voice going from coolly concerned to ironic, "about what I think?"

AMY STARED AT THE MAN WHO had been her husband for all of six hours. Suddenly, she felt she did not know him at all. The Teddy she thought she knew always gave her plenty of space. He respected her decisions. He did not question anything she did or said. He was content to just let her be herself, regardless of other people's expectations, which was why she liked hanging out with him so much.

Letting him know that it was not okay to change tactics now, she offered a tight smile. "Please don't tell me you're playing the husband card."

Teddy's eyebrow went up. "Sorry to disappoint you."

Amy rummaged around in her top dresser drawer for a pair of wool socks. She pulled out a pair decorated with Christmas wreaths. "We never said we would live together right off the bat!"

He sat down beside her on the bed, looking more comfortable now that he was not hunched over slightly to keep from hitting his head on the top of the travel-trailer ceiling. "It was implied."

Amy swallowed and continued pulling on her socks. It wasn't her fault he was so tall and big-boned and muscular. She hadn't ask him to do the physical labor that left his shoulders so taut and broad that he had to turn slightly to make it through the tiny door frames.

"If it was implied," Amy countered, "it was only to you." Finished, she wiggled her sock-clad toes against the carpet…and waited for his rebuttal.

Silence strung out between them.

Just as she expected, he seemed no more apt to back off from his position than she.

He reached over and patted her knee in a manner that was as overly familiar and seductive as it was comforting. "Come on, Amy. People are going to talk enough as it is."

Skin tingling, Amy vaulted to her feet.

Telling herself the fact they were already bickering mightily, after only being hitched a few hours, was not as bad a sign as it might appear, she scoffed, "So now we're worried about appearances?"

Teddy stood, too, seemingly unaware of the unprecedented zing of physical attraction flowing through her.

"Damn straight we are." He placed both hands on her shoulders in a move that felt protective and oddly persuasive. "There are going to be enough raised eyebrows about the fact that we ran off to San Angelo to get hitched without ever going out on a single date." He stared down at her, pausing to let that sink in. His fingers tightened slightly. "If we want to spare ourselves and our families any further discomfort, everything from here on out has to be done the traditional way."

Was it warm in there or what? Amy tugged at the collar of her sweater and, with a slight bend of her knees, extricated herself from his light staying grip. Her skin still tingling, she headed back into the hall to check the thermostat mounted on the wall. Sixty-eight degrees. Not exactly a heat wave.

"Except our marriage isn't traditional," she continued to argue, wishing he weren't so close and warm and didn't smell so good.

"Sure it is." He regarded her with undisguised amusement. "The only thing we won't be doing together right away is having sex, and over time, even that could—actually probably will—change."

Amy's mouth dropped open in surprise at the frank male confidence in his gaze. She hadn't expected the always-easygoing Teddy to be so frank about the difficulties of a platonic marital arrangement.

Aware her heart was pounding, she drew in a stabilizing breath. "You're serious!"

His eyes grew even more serious. He looked interested. and not in the least offended. "Yes," he said bluntly. "I am." He sauntered closer, his gaze drifting over her lazily, before returning with sexy deliberation to her eyes. "You and I are family now. We've got to start acting like one."

If only it were that simple!

Amy marched past him, toward the living room, then recalling she had forgotten her boots, had to go back to the bedroom to rummage through the mismatched stack of footwear in her closet. "I don't have any objections to acting like your wife in social situations." She groaned as she found one red cowgirl boot, and then another, "But that's as far as it's going to go because I am not—I repeat not—sharing a bed with you!"

As she twisted back around to face him, his gaze moved from her denim-clad derriere to her face.

"Then what do you propose we do since we each have only a one-bedroom place?" he asked, leaning casually against the portal. "Purchase twin beds?"

Scowling, Amy sat down on the mattress to pull on her boots, one after the other. And she'd thought Teddy was the one male McCabe who was not completely set on having his own way. How wrong could she have been!

She pointed a finger at his chest. "That might not be a bad idea."

He rolled his eyes in exasperation. "I'm *kidding,* Amy."

"I'm not." She stood up and moved past him, glad the heels of her Western boots had given her an additional three inches. When facing off with him, she needed every bit of height she could get.

Tersely, she reminded him, "We agreed before we said our vows—no sex!"

"Unless," he stated, still looking perfectly at ease, not to mention very handsome, "there comes a time when we both change our minds on that point."

Unbidden, an image of the two of them, naked, between the sheets, entered Amy's mind.

"I told you," she retorted with a lot more patience than she felt, pushing the disturbing image away, "that is very unlikely."

Teddy shrugged, accepting her rejection with the deference of a Texas gentleman, born and bred. "For the immediate future, I agree," he said softly. "We're going to have to get used to living as man and wife in every other way. And *then* see how we feel."

Amy's pulse continued to race. She backed up another step and folded her arms in front of her, like a schoolmarm watching over a bunch of unruly kids at recess. "Which you seem to think will be differently."

He shrugged his broad shoulders, exuding a lazy sexuality she'd never before noticed. Maybe because it had never been aimed at her—even theoretically.

"All I know is that fifty years without sex is a long time, Amy. *Especially* for people like us who are young and healthy and vital. And since we've already promised not to go outside the marriage…"

A tiny thrill went through her. "You'd be willing… to…"

"Be friends with benefits? Eventually? When the time and mood is right? Sure."

He was so calm and matter-of-fact. So confident.

She was a bundle of nerves inside.

She swallowed hard around the knot of emotion in her throat. "Listen, Teddy. I—I don't think I can make love with someone I'm not in love with in that special way."

The familiar gentleness was back in his eyes. "Have you ever tried?"

Reluctantly, with a catch in her voice, she admitted, "Well. No."

"Neither have I," he said. "So how do we know?" He took both her hands in both of his, in that moment looking handsomer than she had ever seen him. "I know we've gotten used to seeing each other in a certain way." He narrowed his gaze and studied her upturned face.

She kept silent, signaling for him to continue.

"But things change, Amy." He paused to tuck a strand of hair behind her ear. "At least they *could* if you would open your mind and your heart to the possibilities…the way I intend to, now that we are husband and wife."

He let go of her, stepped back, hands raised.

"I'm not saying it would happen right away, but…we need to be realistic here," he continued. "There will come a time when the sheer proximity of our situation leads to…temptation. And as responsible adults we need to be prepared for that."

Amy couldn't deny that Teddy exuded sexiness. Or that from time to time she had wondered what it would be like to kiss him. Really kiss him.

She had no idea if he had ever speculated about the same.

She *did* know at their wedding ceremony, when the officiating justice of the peace had said he could kiss the bride, Teddy had given her a brief, friendly peck on the cheek.

She hadn't even expected that much of a caress from him.

Yet if she were honest, she had to admit the deeply romantic side of her had secretly wished for so much more, and been disappointed when Teddy hadn't really planted one on her, even if it was just for show….

The jubilation she had felt then faded, her longtime hope for a baby and family of her very own replaced by uncertainty. Maybe because Amy knew what Teddy didn't—that she had never been as at ease in the bedroom as everyone else seemed to be. Even her experiences with her ex-fiancé had been severely lacking in the physical side of the equation.

Teddy, on the other hand… Well, he had a rep as something of a player among the women he dated….

Figuring as long as they were being brutally honest, they may as well cover this, too, she said awkwardly, "If we were to try…that…and we didn't click, it could wreck everything, Teddy."

The thought of not having him in her life, as her best friend, was unbearable. "I don't want to risk our friendship, never mind our decision to have a family together, on something that might not pan out."

Clearly, he did not share her doubts. "Remember the movie *When Harry Met Sally?*" he asked, flashing a grin her way.

She had dragged him to the theater the previous Valentine's Day for a revival showing when neither of them had dates and hadn't wanted to stay home alone feeling sorry for themselves.

"You're hoping we end up like Harry and Sally," she guessed, warming to the notion. "Going from increasingly close friends-for-life to soul mates and lovers."

Teddy nodded and chucked her on the chin. "And you know what?" A speculative smile curved the corners of his lips. He looked at her as if he had never seen a more beautiful woman in his life. "I think deep down you are, too. Otherwise you wouldn't have married me today."

Chapter Three

"Too bad about last night."

Amy gazed quizzically at her sister, Susie. "What do you mean?"

"It was your first night as husband and wife, and one of Teddy's horses went into labor. That couldn't have been too great."

Amy tried not to think about the irony of the situation. She'd only agreed to go home with Teddy to his ranch for appearances' sake—because she didn't want to let on to anyone how uncertain she already was about this bargain they'd made with each other.

Oh, she still wanted a baby—his baby.

But as for the rest of it…

A marriage based on friendship was going to be much more complicated than she had figured.

Still, figuring boundaries needed to be set, she had packed an overnight bag with her most unsexy flannel pajamas. Only to end up disappointed that she and Teddy hadn't even ended up having dinner together.

Never mind how strange it had felt to sleep in his bed—without him—and leave for work this morning, with only a passing goodbye to him, since he was still busy with the new foal.

It wasn't like this was a real marriage, in the traditional sense. She and Teddy were used to living their own lives, on their own schedules, and having much of their time taken up by the demands of their mutual businesses. More than likely, this was the way it was going to be until a baby came into the picture….

Amy and Susie walked out the back door of the landscape and garden center owned by Susie and headed toward the cargo van Amy used to transport plants.

"You must have felt very let down," Susie continued. "First, you missed out on the big wedding you always wanted, by eloping."

Not to mention the thrill of a life-altering romance, Amy thought.

"Then, as if all that wasn't enough," Susie said, "your first night as husband and wife was a complete bust."

Amy opened up the back door of the dark-green truck, emblazoned with the logo for Laurel Valley Ranch.

Deciding changing the subject was a much safer path to take, Amy pointed out, "You were without a husband last night, too."

The foal had been breech. Susie's husband—and Teddy's triplet brother—Tyler McCabe, was a large-animal vet. He had been called out to the Silverado Ranch to help Teddy with the delivery.

"True," Susie conceded ruefully, watching as Amy set up the loading ramp.

Susie rubbed a hand across her expanding waistline, lovingly protecting the baby inside of her. "But since these days all I want to do is sleep…" Susie walked onto the truck to give a cursory inspection of the red-and-white poinsettia plants and potted baby evergreens Amy was delivering, then signed the clipboard Amy gave her.

"You, on the other hand," Susie continued with another lift of her brow, "are on what should be your honeymoon."

Amy tensed. The sounds of heavy machinery reverberated through the chilly late-November air. She knew the source. Several blocks over, a professional tree crew was removing the live oak that had been struck by lightning and crashed through the chapel roof.

The tree was going to be a loss, Amy knew, but the community chapel would be rebuilt. And in some small way, that knowledge filled her with hope.

Amy got out the wheeled flatbed dolly and began loading plants onto it.

Aware her older sister was waiting for an explanation of some sort, Amy shrugged and turned her glance away from Susie's probing gaze. "My marriage to Teddy isn't like yours and Rebecca's."

Both her sisters were madly in love with the men they had married.

Susie's expression tightened. She tugged on a pair of leather work gloves and lifted the lightweight poinsettia plants, one by one, being careful not to stress her pregnant body. "So I heard."

Amy knew the serious illness Susie had suffered as a teenager had left her more appreciative of life than most, and also more sensitive to others' feelings. Hence, it was no surprise that Susie had picked up on Amy's anxiety and uncertainty, where her own impulsive actions were concerned.

"And you, too, are worried," Amy guessed.

"Everyone is—in both families." Susie watched Amy take the loaded dolly down the ramp to the back door and return with an empty one. "We all know what close friends you and Teddy have been since you were in elementary school together. And we all know how much you both want to be married and have kids."

Here it comes, Amy thought. "But…?"

Susie loaded plants as carefully and sensibly as she did everything else. Pity shone in her eyes. "I can't help but think you're cheating yourselves, not waiting for the love of a lifetime."

Amy sensed an It's-Not-Too-Late-To-Chalk-It-All-Up-To-Holiday-Craziness-And-Get-An-Annulment spiel coming on.

So it wasn't perfect. In fact, far from it. Still, this arrangement she had with Teddy was the key to her getting the family she had always wanted, sooner rather than later.

She and Teddy would work out the details.

Eventually…

That was, if their families would leave them alone to do so!

Amy set her jaw. "If Teddy and I could be sure we'd experience 'true love' with others, don't you think we'd be content to wait? Unfortunately, it would seem the odds are against us finding The One."

Susie straightened. "So you're going to settle for a life with each other instead."

Amy didn't like the way Susie said "settle." She made it sound as if she were stealing crumbs off another's plate, instead of sitting down to a full meal. "It's going to be fine," she reiterated with as much patience and faith as she could muster.

Susie stretched and rubbed her lower back. The shift in her posture made her blossoming pregnancy more apparent. Observing, Amy was filled with a mixture of shared joy—and envy. She didn't like the latter. It made her feel ungrateful somehow. Small and petty.

"If this is so great, then why don't you look happier?" Susie persisted, appearing as determined as their parents the day before to make Amy and Teddy come to their senses and undo what had been done.

Amy took the filled dolly down the ramp and returned with a third empty cart. Gaze averted, she kept her guard up, knowing it would be far too easy to pour out her heart. "I'm stressed out about the holidays." Which was true, as far as it went.

Susie's eyes narrowed skeptically. "You love the holidays."

Amy grimaced and loaded the remaining greenery, slated for Susie's store. "Not so far this year," she said honestly.

"Why? What's going on?" Susie led the way down the ramp, then held the door for Amy.

Amy pushed all three loaded carts into the storeroom, one after another, then followed Susie to her private office. Because the garden center would not be open to the public for another forty-five minutes, they had time to finish their conversation at leisure.

Amy sat down in the chair Susie indicated while her sister poured them each a mug of decaffeinated coffee. "Sheryl was put on bed rest yesterday for the rest of her pregnancy. Her mother can't get in from Chicago to help out until next weekend. Until then, I've given Ed time off to care for her and make sure she doesn't go into early labor again."

"Which leaves you with no help whatsoever."

"Right." Amy stirred creamer in her coffee. This, she could talk at length about. "All my part-time college kids are already back on campus, gearing up for exams."

"And you've got some sort of big delivery coming up,

don't you," Susie recalled, easing into the chair behind her desk.

Amy nodded and rested her mug on her thigh. Warmth transmitted through her jeans. "Two hundred six- to eight-foot Christmas trees have to be delivered to the Wichita Falls Civic Association. The money they earn from the sale is going to provide the Christmas celebration for a local children's home. I'm supposed to deliver them by noon on December 1—which, as it happens, is next Tuesday."

Susie unlocked her desk and pulled out the landscape-design-business checkbook. "How many trees are ready to go so far?" she asked curiously, slipping into business-woman mode.

Amy grimaced, just thinking about what lay ahead. "Sixty-two." It wouldn't have been a problem had her employees been there to help her. But they weren't, and the task ahead was daunting to say the least.

Susie paused to sip her decaf and boot up her computer. "So you've got one hundred and thirty-eight trees—"

"To cut and bundle and load on the ranch cargo truck by Monday evening. Plus—" Amy tried hard not to feel overwhelmed as she sipped her coffee "—twelve dozen cookies to bake for the cookie swap tomorrow evening."

Susie's eyes widened. "That's going to take you *forever* in that tiny oven of yours."

"Tell me about it." But again, it was for a good cause, since the majority of the cookies were going to the nursing homes in the area, to help kick off their holiday seasons.

One eye on her computer screen, Susie rocked back in her chair. "Although, I suppose you could use Teddy's kitchen. He's got double convection ovens."

Amy waved off the offer. "I'll just do it at my place tonight."

Susie stopped typing on the keyboard long enough to ask, "Why?"

"Because we're set to stay at my trailer tonight."

Susie made a face and referred to the delivery numbers on the clipboard. "Why?"

"Because we're alternating domiciles."

Susie emitted a short, strangled laugh. "That's weird."

What was it about older sisters—especially older *married* sisters—that made them think they knew it all?

"No," Amy countered, wishing Susie would hurry up with the process of paying her so she could go. "It's not."

Susie printed out the receipt and took it off the printer. She handed it over, giving Amy a knowing look. "You're keeping one foot out the door. Aren't you?"

"I am not!"

Susie's skepticism only deepened. She sighed and opened her business checkbook. "Is Teddy going to help you with the trees?"

Amy hadn't asked. "He has his own business to run," she said stiffly.

Susie scrawled out figures. "Which can only mean you haven't told him of your dilemma," she chided.

Amy quaffed the rest of her coffee, slightly scalding her throat in the process, and stood. "He doesn't need to help me. I'll figure it out somehow."

Finally, Susie passed the check to Amy. "Well, look, I can't lend you any help today or tomorrow. But we don't have any jobs on Monday morning. So how about I send my landscaping crew over to help you with whatever's left?"

At last. Something was going her way. "That would be great." Amy smiled gratefully. "Thank you. I'll reimburse you for their time."

Susie tapped her pen against her chin. "What about delivering the trees? What are you going to do about that?"

They both knew Ed usually handled any long hauls. With Sheryl so close to giving birth, that would not be possible, either.

"I'm going to drive the truck up early Tuesday morning," Amy said.

Susie looked shocked. "By yourself?"

"Yes." Amy stuck the check on the clipboard, on top of the receipt. "I'll have plenty of help on the other end to unload."

Susie stood to walk her out, lacing a sisterly arm about Amy's waist. "I hope you don't get stuck up there."

Amy tucked the clipboard beneath her arm and rocked forward on her toes. "The bad weather is not supposed to hit until Wednesday morning."

"You know how fast that can change." Susie watched as Amy climbed back up into the cab. "Especially that close to the Oklahoma border."

"I'm sure I'll be fine." Amy fit her keys into the ignition and fastened her seat belt. "But if it looks bad, I'll stay in a hotel."

Susie remained concerned. "Promise me you won't try to beat a storm."

Amy rolled her eyes. "Have I ever gotten caught out in one yet?"

"No, by the grace of heaven, you haven't," Susie admitted with a reluctant twist of her lips. "But there's always a first time."

Amy wagged a finger at her. "You're supposed to be worrying about that baby you're carrying, Suze, not me."

Susie held up her hands in surrender. "I can't help it. I'm your big sister. Always will be."

And family, Amy knew, took care of family. Which was exactly why she wasn't telling Teddy of her dilemma. She didn't want him thinking that as her husband he needed to interfere in her Laurel Valley Ranch business.

AMY DELIVERED MORE POINSETTIA plants and decorative cuttings of fresh holly and evergreen branches to area florists and stopped at the grocery store on the way home. As usual at that time of day, the lines were long. Made worse by the fact that everyone in town had heard about her marriage.

"That's some husband you've lassoed yourself." Maisy, the store manager, winked.

The clerk ringing up Amy's groceries agreed. "You've got the envy of quite a few women in this town."

Unfortunately, Amy didn't feel lucky. She felt foolish. Naive. And less in-the-spirit-of-Christmas than ever as she walked out of the store and drove back to her ranch.

Hoping she'd have some time to pull herself together before facing her new husband again, she turned into the lane and stopped at what she saw. Teddy was already there. Once again, taking over in a way he never had during all the years they had been "just friends."

Temper simmering at the assumptions he had obviously made, she parked her truck next to the barn, got out with the grocery bags in hand and crossed the gravel.

He'd had a shower since she'd seen him last, and the fragrance of soap and shaving cream clung to his skin. His layered reddish-brown hair curled up slightly where it brushed the nape of his neck.

Despite the chill in the air, he wore only a tan chamois shirt, long-sleeved undershirt and jeans. His sheepskin-lined suede jacket and hat lay next to the open toolbox on the ground beside the stoop.

Teddy stopped hammering long enough to give her a welcoming smile.

Ignoring the way her heart skittered in response, Amy stopped just short of him. She made no effort to keep the incredulity out of her voice. "What are you doing?"

He kept right on hammering, easy as you please. Every *thwack* stretched the fabric across his brawny shoulders and delineated the bunched muscles in his chest. His jeans were doing equally amazing things for his thighs and butt, and despite her earlier promise to keep their relationship strictly platonic for now, Amy felt her mouth go dry.

"Exactly what it looks like," he said, as if it were the most natural thing in the world for him to be undertaking. On *her* ranch, no less! "I'm installing a satellite dish."

Amy drew a deep, bolstering breath. She dropped the grocery sacks in the grass and struggled to keep her emotions under control.

"I can see that," she said with a great deal more patience than she actually felt. "Why?"

Teddy straightened slowly. As he faced her, his superior height seemed more pronounced than ever. "Because you only get two channels out here with a rabbit-ear antenna, and there's no cable this far out in the country." Ignoring her irritation, he picked up the instructions and scanned them briefly.

Amy stomped closer and glared at him. "I don't need more channels."

He put the paper down, laconic as ever, and picked up a wire. "There's the rub, darlin'." He paused to give her a long, telling look. "I do."

Darlin'! When did he call her *"darlin'"*? Teddy called his girlfriends that. Never her.

Aware it was all she could do not to kick him in the shin, Amy doubled back and picked up her groceries. "For what?"

Teddy mugged comically, as if the answer to that were obvious. "Football play-offs. The Super Bowl. Not to mention the Dallas Stars or the Mavericks."

Fortunately, he had satellite at his ranch. "I don't watch hockey, Teddy. Or basketball, either." And she detested football!

His teeth flashed white in an infuriating smile. She was pretty sure he knew he was irritating the heck out of her and was determined to keep right on doing it. "That's the beauty of it," he told her in a soft, sexy voice that did funny things to her insides. He tapped her on the chest. "*You* don't have to."

Now, that was debatable, Amy thought, given the tiny space in her travel-trailer.

"I'll hear it," she complained.

Teddy shrugged his broad shoulders. "If it bothers you," he said, looking no closer to backing down than she was, "I'll get headphones for the TV."

"Or just watch at your place," Amy suggested with a sweetness meant to set his teeth on edge.

His attention focused more on his task than on her, Teddy attached the wire to the dish. "I'd be glad to do that," he responded amiably, "if you'd come to your senses and agree to let us live at the Silverado one hundred percent of the time."

So that was what this was about!

Amy exhaled loudly. "I explained why it wouldn't be good to do that."

"Actually—" his expression mirrored her exasperation "—you didn't. But I'll let that one pass for now. In the meantime," he said, looking around with male satisfaction, his lips twitching upward into a smile, "thanks to my work here, I've got many more channels for us both to watch. And," he added, "another surprise inside, too."

With the deeply inbred courtesy of a Texas gentleman, he walked ahead to hold the door.

Amy stubbornly stayed right where she was. She wasn't sure she wanted any more "surprises," if they were of the ilk that he was assuming the role of head of the household and taking over her life.

"What else did you do?" she demanded.

Teddy came back down the steps and removed the grocery sacks—which were getting heavier by the minute—from her hands.

"Why are you so wary all of a sudden?" he asked, beginning to look a little irked, too.

Amy huffed. "Why are you so…bossy…suddenly?"

A frown etched deep grooves on either side of his sensual lips. "I'm not bossy."

Hah! She begged to differ. "It looks like you're trying to take over here."

He shook off her displeasure and nudged her toward the stoop. "You'll feel better when you have a hot meal."

Amy only wished she could sit down and eat dinner and watch some TV. Not sports. But maybe something else she didn't get, like the Home and Garden or the Cooking channel.

Unfortunately, she had cookies to bake. "That's going to have to wait," she warned, getting weary just thinking about it.

"Not necessarily," Teddy replied smugly.

Before she could formulate a response, a high-pitched beeping began inside her trailer.

"What the…?" Amy said, dread springing up inside her as she recognized the sound. "That's my smoke alarm!"

Looking equally stunned and on edge, Teddy dropped her grocery sacks. Together, they raced for the door. Teddy got there first and swung it open. Choking swirls of dark gray smoke poured out.

"What in the world…?" Amy swore, waving the smoke away so she could see. She hadn't left anything on that she knew of.

Only Teddy seemed to have a clue how this could be happening.

"Stay there…" He pushed her back and entered the trailer ahead of her.

He charged past the sofa and table, straight to the tiny galley kitchen. Muttering a string of words that weren't fit for polite company, he jerked open the miniscule oven door. More smoke poured out, along with a noxious smell.

Grabbing a pair of mitts, he pulled a charred black pie pan from the oven and set it on top of the stove.

Amy grabbed a chair, climbed on top of it and yanked the smoke alarm from the wall. Blessed silence followed.

Teddy leaned across the kitchen sink to open a window. Then another. While Amy could only stare at the ruins in mounting disbelief.

OKAY. THIS WAS DEFINITELY NOT going the way he had planned, Teddy thought, staring into Amy's brown eyes. But then, so far nothing about their hasty marriage was meeting expectations.

Which didn't mean he couldn't set things to right. Eventually.

He watched her pick up an aluminum cookie sheet and wave smoke toward the open window with big imperious motions that only seemed to underscore what a moron she thought he was.

Glad she wasn't crying—crying would have made things worse—he explained calmly, "I wanted to surprise you."

Her expression remaining unreadable, Amy frowned at the foot of countertop she had on either side of her two-burner stove. "You've done that, all right."

Okay, she was mad. But she had a right to be. Figuring she might as well get it all out, he prodded her deliberately, "Now what's wrong?"

Amy looked at him as if to say, *You even have to ask?* Then she pointed at the carcass of the rotisserie chicken on the cutting board, the empty containers of cream and chicken broth, and the sack of frozen vegetables, before turning to the place where he'd unrolled the refrigerated pie dough.

He shrugged off the messy countertop, not sure why that should be so grating. "I clean up *after* I eat," he explained mildly, knowing it was the only time-efficient way to proceed. "That way I only have to do it once."

"Clearly," she said, as if to a four-year-old.

Wishing she didn't look so hot and bothered and totally hypercritical, he grabbed the kitchen wastebasket and began piling things into the plastic sack inside of it. He hadn't expected Amy to be the kind of wife who would be on his case about mundane things. Or really, anything. Not that she didn't have a right to be ticked off over the ruined meal. He was disappointed about that, too…and hungry, to boot.

Out of the corner of his eye, he saw her run both her hands through her short blond hair, rumpling the wind-tossed strands even more. Her cute-as-a-pixie features were tinged an emotional pink. He had the oddest desire to take her in his arms and hold her till the tension in her slender body dissipated. Not that he imagined she would warm to such an action, either.

Teddy exhaled his frustration. "I don't know what happened to the chicken pot pie." He checked the oven's temperature dial. It was right where it should be. "I've made it dozens of times. I've never burned it. Never." Stymied, he looked inside the oven.

Worse than the charred black remains sitting on the stovetop was the mess it had left inside the stove. The pie had obviously boiled over and burned a horrendous black mess on the bottom of her oven.

"You should have asked me first," Amy said dully, running her hands through her hair yet again. Abruptly, her anger faded and she looked like she was going to start crying.

Feeling worse than ever for the screwup, Teddy finished dumping things into the trash and looked around for a dishrag. "I was trying to make up for last night. I know that was an inauspicious start to our marriage, at best."

"It's nothing compared to this." Two tears slid down Amy's cheeks. Her body limp with the weariness that came from a long day at work, she sagged against the opposite wall.

The need to protect her pouring through him, Teddy held up a reassuring hand. "I'll clean this up. Though I still don't know why our dinner burned."

Amy rubbed the moisture from her face and seemed to pull herself together, every bit as suddenly as she had started to fall apart. She took a deep breath that lifted the soft swell of her full breasts. "My oven doesn't calibrate properly, Teddy." She looked him in the eye. "It heats one hundred and fifty degrees above whatever the dial indicates."

"So three hundred fifty degrees was…?"

"Five hundred degrees."

Teddy swore. "No wonder it burned." He was lucky he hadn't set the whole place on fire while blithely installing a satellite dish she didn't seem to want any more than his company.

Spine stiff, Amy walked back outside and retrieved her groceries. Knowing a change of scene would help, Teddy suggested, "We could forget cooking and go out to dinner."

Again, Amy shook her head, discounting both his invitation and his help. "I don't have time. I have to bake twelve dozen cookies tonight."

Taking charge, Teddy replied, "Then you're going to have to do it at my place."

AMY WOULD HAVE LIKED TO turn down Teddy's offer. She couldn't. She had to honor her commitment to the organizers of the cookie swap. So for the second night in a row, she packed a bag, got in her pickup truck and drove to the Silverado while Teddy stayed behind to finish the satellite dish and clean up.

Once at his place, she couldn't help but compare his abode to hers. At just under fifteen hundred square feet, his one-story, sand-colored brick ranch house was roughly three times the square footage of her trailer.

Dark-brown shutters adorned the windows and a covered porch lent shelter to the solid oak front door. The exterior landscaping was sparse, leaving the impression that the person who lived here hadn't gone to much trouble to add plants or trees, although the lawn was thick and well maintained.

Inside the abode was a different story.

Over the ten years Teddy had resided in the 1980s home, he had slowly but surely redone it, ripping out carpet and putting wide-plank oak flooring throughout. The main area of the house was completely open, revealing a state-of-the-art kitchen with a six-burner stove and double ovens, microwave and sub-zero refrigerator. Cushiony leather stools lined the long granite counter. A long wooden table with Windsor chairs sat next to the bay window overlooking the back patio.

Toward the front of the house, a great room with cathedral ceiling sported a huge beige stone fireplace and mantel. A comfortable sectional sofa that seated seven fronted a big wooden coffee table. An entertainment center featuring a digital stereo and large-screen plasma TV was flanked by book-filled shelves on either side.

To the rear of the house, there was a master bedroom, complete with king-size bed. He had knocked out one of the bedrooms in order to expand the master bath into a beautiful, luxurious retreat, complete with marble counters and double sinks, glass-walled shower and whirlpool soaking tub.

An office and another half bath completed the abode.

The house was decorated primarily in the same beige and brown of the outside of the ranch house. It was definitely a bachelor's lair. In many ways as unsuited for a family as her own tiny one-person trailer, a fact that weighed heavily on her as she rummaged through his kitchen, looking for everything she needed.

Yet they had to live somewhere, until they figured out how—and where—they were going to expand their living quarters into something suitable for the both of them and any children they had.

That being the case, if she were smart, Amy thought as she slid the butter into the microwave to soften, she would simply move her things over here and be done with it. Make life simpler for both of them.

So why couldn't she do that?

What really had her keeping one foot out the door?

"SMELLS GREAT IN HERE," Teddy said, two hours later. He walked in, take-out pizza and a big bottle of Amy's favorite diet cola in hand.

Pleased his earlier irritation with her had faded as surely as hers with him, she smiled. "It's the gingerbread cookies."

He set their dinner down and closed the distance between them, the familiar kindness in his green eyes. Relief filtered through her, as intense and all-consuming as her earlier anger.

"About earlier—" he said in a deeply apologetic voice that sent shivers over her skin.

Amy swallowed. It was ridiculous, how happy and relieved she was to see him, to realize their "marriage" wasn't over before it had even begun.

Aware her pulse was jumping, she looked into his eyes. "I'm really sorry, Teddy. I don't know what got into me. All I know is I overreacted."

"Not really." He took both her hands in his and squeezed them, in the familiar way of an old friend. "I made one heck of a mess in your kitchen. And I installed a satellite dish without your permission—which I'll take out tomorrow if you want."

Amy'd had enough time to think while she worked in

his kitchen. If this was going to work, she realized that she had to be willing to give some ground, too. She couldn't expect Teddy to make all the sacrifices and adjustments while she kept her life exactly the same.

"No." She tilted her face up to his and looked into his eyes. "You're right. If you're going to be spending time there, too, you need to be comfortable, Teddy."

She could live with televised sports if it meant she could have the family and children she had always wanted.

She just wasn't quite sure how she was going to live with him.

Before they'd said their *I do's,* when they had just been friends, sex—or the possibility of it—had never been an issue with them. Now it seemed to hang in the air at every turn.

Making her realize what a "catch" he was.

Handsome, athletic, kind and generous to a fault. It didn't take much imagination to realize he would be a handful in bed.

If they ever got to bed…

Oblivious to the amorous nature of her thoughts, he let go of her hands, and went to the cupboard to get two plates. "You'll be happy to know the oven and kitchen at your place are spic and span, the burnt smell is gone, and the smoke alarm is back in working order."

"Thanks." Aware how small even his spacious kitchen seemed with the two of them in it, Amy flushed self-consciously. "I should have warned you about the oven." She filled two glasses with ice, grabbed the soda and met him at the table.

He reached out to help her with her chair. "You would've had you known I was planning to cook."

They exchanged awkward smiles and sat down

opposite each other. Amy couldn't help but feel the tension reverberating between them. Taking in the way his gaze drifted, however briefly, to her breasts, before moving back to her face, it dawned on her that she was not the only one thinking about sex.

"Things have to get better," Amy said hopefully.

He agreed with an amused lift of his brow. "Can't get much worse than they've been thus far," he drawled.

More silence fell, slightly more comfortable this time.

Amy studied his face. "What's happening to us?" she whispered, resting her chin on her upturned palm. "We've been friends forever and it's never been this…"

"Awkward?" Teddy opened the pizza box, handed her a slice.

"And awful." She paused. Figuring the more they talked about it, got everything out in the open, the better their chances for a more harmonious existence, she said, "We're fighting like cats and dogs."

Teddy kicked back in his chair, his expression pensive. He tilted his head to one side. "Can't be the wedding rings. Can it?"

"I don't know." She studied the plain gold band on her left hand, then returned his searching glance, happy their old camaraderie was returning. She didn't mind facing problems, as long as they faced them together. She picked a slice of pepperoni off the top of the pizza and bit her lip. "What do you think?"

He looked down at the gold band on his left hand. "A case of post-wedding jitters?" he proposed.

Amy brightened. "Due to poor pre-ceremony planning?" she mused.

"And familial disapproval," he added.

"No kidding!" Amy heaved a heartfelt sigh. There had

been an uncommon amount of stress in the past thirty-six hours. Clearly, she and Teddy were just reacting to that. Once things settled down…

"It'll pass," Teddy predicted.

It was going to have to, Amy thought, picking up her pizza and taking a satisfying bite. She couldn't live with this much tension and anxiety. Not and be happy or anywhere even close to it.

Chapter Four

"I'm glad you're here," Luke Carrigan told Teddy at the chapel the next afternoon, where construction of a new roof was under way. Fifty men had volunteered to help the professional roofers and structural engineers in charge of the reconstruction and repair efforts.

Luke was manning one of the power saws, cutting lumber to size. Teddy had been assigned the task of carefully measuring and marking each piece.

"I've been wanting to talk to you," Luke continued.

Teddy had figured as much. He couldn't blame him. Were he Amy's father, he would have wanted to chat with his new son-in-law, too.

"So how's it going so far?" Luke asked.

"We're still settling in," Teddy said finally. "But we had fun last night." It had almost seemed like old times. Before the rush to the altar…when the only thing on their minds had been having a good time. "I helped her make gingerbread cookies." Then Amy had slept on the sofa, and he'd taken his bed. He was bleary-eyed from lying awake half the night, wondering where the desire to kiss her…really kiss her…had come from.

"So you're living where right now?"

"We're alternating houses at the moment." Tonight they were going to be at the trailer. They were still trying to figure out where he was going to sleep—on a sofa that was a good two feet too short for him, or in the double bed that was also too small for his six-foot-four frame.

Luke paused to study Teddy. "Where's Amy now?"

"She had work to do on her ranch, then this evening, she's going to the cookie swap."

"You won't see her…"

"Till I get done here."

"I saw she had signed up to work on the cleaning and painting of the interior of the church later this week."

Teddy nodded. "We both did."

It meant a lot to both of them, getting the community chapel restored before the Christmas holidays.

Luke lined up another piece of lumber and ran it through the saw. "I guess it's no secret Amy's mother and I remain concerned."

"No, sir, it isn't." Teddy was pretty sure his parents still felt the same way. They just hadn't had a chance to corner him yet.

Luke carried the wood over to the growing pile of cut lumber, then paused to get a drink from the water bottle he'd brought with him. "Had you two told us of your plans, Meg and I would have moved heaven and earth to stop you from making such a big mistake. Especially," he continued gravely, giving Teddy no chance to interrupt, "since you are the reason Amy hasn't found anyone to spend the rest of her life with, and vice versa."

This was news. "How do you figure that?" Teddy asked. He'd never tried to keep Amy from dating anyone. Heck, he'd encouraged her to go out with other guys, just as she had urged him to date all likely prospects that came his way. It wasn't his fault—or hers—that none of the people either of them had dated had come close to measuring up.

Luke clapped a fatherly hand on Teddy's shoulder. "You two have gotten so close over the years, spent so much time together. No one new coming into either of your lives can compete with that kind of intimacy. Not," he added quickly, "that it's all your fault. Amy's experience with Ken left her wary of giving her heart to anyone again. That's why I'd held back on trying to set her up with any potential suitors just yet."

Teddy eyed him curiously. "You don't think she considered marriage to me a risk?"

"I think she figured she would be safe as long as her heart wasn't involved with you, the way it was with Ken."

Teddy pushed away his unease. "Why did they end the engagement?" he asked.

Luke looked stunned. "She didn't tell you?"

"Amy and I made a pact early on never to give each other the details on the people we were dating." For reasons Teddy had never been able to put a finger on—it just hadn't felt right, talking to Amy about the women in his life…or hearing about the men in hers. So they'd steadfastly avoided the topic.

Teddy shrugged, admitting, "All Amy ever said was that 'Ken wasn't the man she thought he was.' I know the breakup left her feeling embarrassed and humiliated, but not a lot more." Amy had never wanted to talk about it further. And he hadn't wanted to push her.

Belatedly, Teddy realized he probably should have been more insistent. Particularly if Ken was the reason Amy was still so closed off, as her father seemed to be indicating.

Luke gave Teddy a frank, man-to-man look. "You'll have to ask her if you want to know more than that. It's not my story to tell. In the meantime, I expect you and my daughter are both stubborn enough to want to see this marriage through, but when it ends—and it will end, Teddy, because no union can survive without a foundation of deep, abiding *romantic* love—then I expect you to do the honorable thing and let my daughter go. And make it a clean break. So you and she will both have a chance with someone else."

Teddy wanted to disregard everything Amy's father had said. He couldn't. As close as he and Amy were, there was still a lot he wanted—needed—to learn about the woman he had married.

Unfortunately, by the time work on the chapel roof wrapped up and he got back to Laurel Valley Ranch, it was ten o'clock. Amy was already fast asleep on the living room sofa. Curled up on her side, one hand pressed to her cheek, the other tucked beneath the pillow, her golden curls tousled…she looked young and innocent and incredibly sexy.

Aware the trailer had taken on a chill, the way it did every night when the sun went down, he got a second blanket off the back of the sofa and spread it over her. She shifted slightly, sighed softly and drifted right back into sleep.

Surprised by the tenderness he felt, Teddy picked up his overnight bag and walked soundlessly to the rear of the trailer.

By the time he had stepped into the shower, he had an ache that wouldn't quit. An ache that had little to do with friendship and everything to do with the fact Amy was now his wife.

A piece of paper…a couple of words said in a judge's office…shouldn't make a difference.

But it did.

And Teddy didn't know what in blazes he was going to do about that.

For Teddy, morning came all too soon.

Stiff and sore from a night bent like a pretzel, he pushed back the covers and struggled to get out of bed. As he made his way to the miniscule bathroom, he realized the trailer was awfully quiet.

He followed the aroma of freshly brewed coffee into the kitchen and his spirits sank. The blankets on the sofa were folded neatly. The coffee carafe sat on the kitchen counter, beside a note scrawled in Amy's hand.

Teddy,
    I really need to sleep here tonight. So if you wouldn't mind… We'll double up at your place after that, to make up for it.
    Amy.

Teddy scowled. He'd had more time with his wife when they weren't married.

Amy felt a little guilty for repeatedly ducking out on Teddy over the weekend. Not that she could have helped with the roofing of the chapel—that was clearly a guys-only job, with only guys volunteering. And she had needed to work. But she could have stayed around this morning, to have a cup of coffee with him, or at least say good morning before she took off for town, to get some more bundling mesh for the trees she was cutting.

She hadn't, because the thought of furthering the intimacy between them left her feeling all jittery inside. They'd had no trouble keeping to established boundaries when they were friends. Now the same rules seemed oddly confining. The thought of setting new ones was even more daunting.

Fortunately, the note Teddy had left for her on the kitchen counter indicated he had client appointments at his ranch and wouldn't be home until eight or nine that evening. He advised her not to wait dinner on him; he'd grab a sandwich at his place.

Realizing she should be relieved not to have to worry about doing anything wifely when she was exhausted from a day spent cutting and bundling trees, Amy made a sandwich for herself. She had just washed her dishes and retreated to her bedroom when Teddy strode into the trailer, looking freshly showered and shaved. And loaded for bear. "What's this I hear about you driving a load of trees to Wichita Falls by yourself tomorrow?" he demanded.

So much for the boundaries they'd previously had in place.

Deciding it was high time she got cleaned up, too, Amy grabbed her pajamas and a pair of panties from the top dresser drawer. "Who told you?"

Teddy leaned a shoulder against the door frame, watching as she maneuvered the foot of space between the bed and the only other piece of furniture in the room. "Tyler— who heard it from Susie."

"Figures," Amy grumbled. Being the baby of the family made everyone think they had to manage her life for her. She had figured that would change as she got older. To her chagrin, it hadn't.

"You know there's a fierce winter storm from Colorado headed our way."

What was it about him that made her trailer feel so small and close, instead of cozy and warm, whenever he was here with her? It was more than just the sheer size of him. It was the way he looked at her since they'd said their vows. Like he wanted to possess her...

Aware she was letting her thoughts slide into forbidden territory again, Amy went back to her dresser and added a bra to the bundle of nightclothes in her hand.

"The ice and snow is not supposed to hit Laramie." She had to kneel on the bed, which pressed up against the opposite wall, to open the sliding closet doors.

Teddy edged closer. The masculine fragrance of his soap and cologne inundated her. "But all reports predict it will hit Wichita Falls."

Amy plucked a robe from a hanger, and a clean towel and washcloth from the shelf. "Not until tomorrow evening, at which point I will already be safely back in Laramie."

Teddy stepped aside to let her pass. "What time are you leaving?"

Amy set her clothing on the top of the clothes hamper. "Dawn." She had promised the trees would be there by noon at the latest. This would give her plenty of time.

Teddy watched as she rubbed cleansing lotion onto her face. "Who's going to unload the truck?"

Amy dampened a washcloth and washed off the remains of the day. "The members of the civic club. They're supposed to have a dozen people there, so it shouldn't take long. I can collect my paycheck and be on my way." Finished, she layered toothpaste onto a brush.

Teddy frowned as she brushed and rinsed. "I still don't like it."

Amy bent to take off her wool socks. His presence kept her from disrobing any further. "It's not really up to you to like or dislike it." Hand to the center of his chest, she pushed him gently back into the narrow hall, between the bedroom and kitchen. Her palm tingled from the solid warmth of him. She dropped her hand and stepped back, so she was just inside the bath. Before he could continue, she added, "And if you say you're my husband now, I really am going to lose it."

Teddy grinned unrepentantly. "Is that so?"

Aware her pulse was racing, Amy nodded. "I managed just fine without you all these years. You don't need to step in and run my life now."

His expression gentled. "I'll feel better if I'm with you."

Unsolicited orders were easy to ignore. Tenderness was much harder to fight. Amy drew a stabilizing breath. "You have your own business to run."

"Nothing that can't be managed by my part-time help." This time, he held up a hand to cut her off. "I'm going with you tomorrow, Amy. End of story. Now, where are we going to sleep tonight?"

FIFTEEN MINUTES LATER, Teddy lay in Amy's double bed, listening to the shower running. Funny, he had never had much trouble ignoring Amy's soft curves and silky skin when they had just been friends. Now, as he lay in sheets and blankets scented with the unique fragrance of her, it was much harder to stay immune to her delectable presence.

Had he insisted they sleep at his place, he could have stretched out on the sectional sofa and given her his king-size bed.

Knowing how important it was to her to maintain her independence, he had respected her request and come here to sleep. Again. Since there was no way he could get his body onto her sofa, he had ended up scrunched up on the double bed, which was still too small by half. Hoping yet another uncomfortable night would show her the wisdom of sleeping at his place from here on out, he closed his eyes.

The water in the bathroom shut off.

He heard Amy moving around, knew she was toweling off.

It took forever for her to dress.

Blow-dry her hair.

Emerge from the bathroom, smelling like the perfumed soap and shampoo she used, and tiptoe toward the other end of the small trailer.

Aware his body was reacting in a way it shouldn't, he turned onto his side. Given the way he was aching, it was going to be a long night.

Eventually, Teddy went to sleep.

When the alarm went off, he dressed and went out to transfer the necessities from his pickup to her cargo truck.

Amy climbed behind the wheel, a thermos of coffee, a bag of granola bars and apples, and two thermal mugs in her arms. She cast a skeptical look at the boxes he'd stowed behind the seat. "What's all this?"

"Survival gear."

Her pretty eyes widened. "You're kidding."

Teddy shrugged and climbed into the cab beside her. "Never hurts to be prepared. There's a lot of desolate road between here and Wichita Falls."

Scoffing, Amy fit the key into the ignition. "We're not going to need that stuff."

"Of course we're not," he teased. "We'd only need it if we didn't have it."

She considered that. "True."

Trying not to appear as antsy as he felt, he settled into the passenger seat. "You want to split the driving?" He wasn't used to taking the passive role. Particularly when he was with her.

"No." Amy's chin took on a familiar, stubborn tilt. "I can do it."

Teddy forced himself not to exhale in exasperation. "If you change your mind…"

"I'll let you know."

The morning passed quickly. Although the weather reports remained dire, the pavement was dry when they reached Wichita Falls. However, the clouds were a deep, troubling gray-white.

Luckily, the trees were unloaded quickly and Amy was paid.

By three that afternoon, they were on their way back.

Shortly after, the rain began.

"Maybe we should just err on the side of caution and get a room somewhere," Teddy said, studying the sky.

"And get stuck here for who knows how many days if this turns to ice? I don't think so. We're moving away from the storm. I think we should continue. Besides, it's just rain."

"Now." Teddy pointed to the digital numbers on her dashboard that indicated it was currently thirty-three degrees outside. "If the temperature dips a point or two, we could be dealing with freezing rain or sleet."

"By the time that happens, we'll be well out of harm's way," Amy predicted.

Not necessarily, since the storm was moving in a southerly direction, from the west, and they were headed southwest.

"At least let me drive," Teddy said, aware they were still a good five hours from home.

Amy gripped the wheel with both hands, her attention firmly on the road. "Your job is to ride shotgun. That's it."

Was this what it was going to be like to be married to her? Amy seemed to be holding on to her autonomy with all her might. And while Teddy understood that—he, too, had an independent streak a mile wide—he also knew that marriage required compromise. Thus far, Amy hadn't demonstrated much of an inclination to meet him halfway on anything, never mind allow him to protect and care for her in the traditional way husbands cared for their wives.

He found that frustrating as hell.

"Don't worry," Amy promised, completely misreading the reason behind his concern. "We'll stop and get some dinner when we get far enough away from all this."

TWO HOURS LATER, AMY GLARED at Teddy from across the table. He'd barely spoken to her since they entered the restaurant. Worse, he was so edgy he was making her tense. "Would you stop fidgeting and looking at your watch?" she asked irritably.

"Can't help it." The look he gave her mirrored her mood to a T. "I'd rather be driving. Actually—" he held up a hand and corrected before she could comment "— I'd rather be checked into a hotel room."

That was the last thing they needed. Especially when the idea of the two of them sequestered in a hotel room together, waiting for the winter storm to pass, immediately conjured up forbidden images of hot, passionate sex....

Forcing herself to stop her wayward thoughts—hadn't

notions like that gotten her into trouble in the past?—
Amy turned her gaze toward the Christmas tree in the
lobby of the truck stop.

Although carols were playing on the sound system, and
peppermint ice cream pie was on the menu, it still didn't
feel like Christmas to her. Amy forked up some turkey and
dressing, glad for their first hot meal of the day. "Hold on
to your britches," she grumbled. "I'm eating as fast as I
can."

He brightened. "You could take it with us and eat it in
the truck if you'd let me drive."

It would be so easy to lean on him. It would also be a
bad precedent to set, unless she wanted him telling her
what to do, every day for the rest of her life. Amy went
back to glaring at him. "Just because I don't inhale my
food at the speed of light the way you do…"

He arched a brow, obviously fed up with all the waiting
around, even though they'd only been in the restaurant for
twenty minutes or so.

"I'm going to get some coffee for our thermos." He
left the table.

Amy looked out the window. It was raining pretty hard.
Now that the sun had gone down, the temperature was
dropping, too. She hurried up, despite her early admoni-
tion not to be worried by all the alarmist predictions on
the airwaves. By the time she emerged from the ladies'
room, the check had been paid. Full thermos in hand,
Teddy was ready to go.

As they walked back out to the truck, icy rain pelted
their faces.

It hadn't been coming down anywhere near this hard
when they had stopped for dinner half an hour ago. In fact,
it had barely been raining at all.

Her foot slid on the slick pavement as she approached the driver's side. He caught her.

She had only to look into his eyes to know what he was thinking.

They could spend the night here.

They wouldn't have a bed, or any privacy, but they'd have heat, food, bathrooms. And he'd be looking at her with that I-told-you-this-was-a-bad-idea gaze all night long.

"I want to keep going."

His expression remained impassive. "You're the boss. It's your call."

Amy didn't like the sound of that. There weren't supposed to be any bosses in their marriage between friends. She stuck her hands in the pockets of her down jacket. "No need to be sarcastic."

He kept the steadying hand on her elbow and gave her a chivalrous boost up into the cab. "Be grateful I'm still this circumspect."

Amy scowled and started the truck. To her relief, the dashboard indicated the outside temperature was still thirty-three degrees.

She went over to gas up, and then turned the truck back onto the two-lane highway. "It's thirty-four miles to the next town," she said. "If it looks any worse by the time we get there, we'll stop there for the night."

Teddy nodded.

To Amy's relief, the next fifteen miles were fine, although she drove very slowly and carefully, just to be on the safe side.

It was only when they got into an area that was as desolate as the desert, that the temperature began to dip even more. And that was when the road got really slick.

One minute they were cruising along, easy as you please, the next they were skating across a sheet of black ice. Fishtailing, then spinning all the way around, before bumping across a cactus-riddled field and coming to an abrupt halt.

IT TOOK A GOOD FIFTEEN seconds after they stopped for Amy to catch her breath. Recovering, she gripped the wheel hard with both hands and stepped on the gas. The truck went exactly nowhere.

She tried again and was rewarded with a spinning sound and a sinking truck.

"Try rocking it back and forth," Teddy suggested.

She did…to no avail.

She eased off the gas, frustration knotting her gut, and shifted the truck into Park. Swearing softly beneath her breath, Amy unfastened her seat belt and jumped down from the cab. Teddy followed her onto the ground. It took only a moment to see what the problem was. The truck's front wheels were stuck in the mud.

Amy sighed, as the freezing precipitation continued to rain down on them. "We're not going to be able to get out of this, are we?"

"Not until it stops. Which should be by daylight."

"Lovely."

She climbed back in the truck and turned off the ignition.

Silence surrounded them, broken only by the pelting sounds of the ice hitting the windshield and top of the cab.

Teddy reached around behind them. He brought out a couple of wool blankets and draped them over their laps.

He lit a candle, stuck it inside a hurricane globe and set it on the dash. "This candle will keep it fifty degrees in here, all on its own."

The heat of his body would keep it warmer than that.

Amy ran a hand over her eyes and slumped down in her seat. "You can say I told you so any time now," she grumbled, feeling incredibly foolish.

Teddy draped his arm along the back of the bench seat and turned toward her. Using the pressure of his hand on her shoulder, he urged her out from behind the wheel, not stopping until they were sitting side by side in the center of the wide bench seat. "When in our many years of friendship have I ever said I told you so to you?" he asked her in a deep, kind voice.

"There's a first time for everything," Amy replied miserably.

He shifted, getting more comfortable, too. His leg nudged hers beneath the blankets. "Are we talking about me now or your ex-fiancé?"

Amy shut her eyes and tipped her head back until it rested against the seat. "You know I don't talk about that."

He pulled her deeper into the curve of his arm. "Maybe it's time you do."

Needing to see the expression on his face, Amy opened her eyes and looked at him. "You first, then. 'Cause you never said why you and Vanna broke it off, either."

For a long moment, Amy thought Teddy was going to put up the usual smoke screen into his most private thoughts about all members of the opposite sex. Then something in his gaze shifted, became more intimate still. With the change in his mood, a new peace stole over the cab of the truck. His sensual lips curving ruefully, he murmured, "Vanna said the thrill was gone. Our life together was too ordinary. I was too ordinary. Too nice."

How could someone be too nice? Amy wondered, incensed.

"There weren't enough fireworks. Vanna needed drama and I couldn't…or to hear her talk—wouldn't—give it to her. So she handed me back my engagement ring and left." Teddy reached over and absently squeezed Amy's hand.

"At the time I was pretty hurt," he continued reflectively. "Now I realize she did us both a favor. Because if there's one thing I've learned about myself, Amy, is that I like ordinary. I probably even like dull as long as life is one smooth ride."

Amy blinked. "Wow."

He grinned, looking relieved to finally have that off his chest, gave her hand another squeeze and let it go.

He gave her another nudge. "Your turn."

Hoping the candlelight hid her blush, Amy drew an enervating breath. "It's embarrassing."

Teddy scoffed, not about to let her off the hook. "And mine wasn't?"

He had a point.

Reluctantly, Amy plunged into her own confession. "I found out I wasn't Ken's only fiancée. He had another one in his hometown of Boise, Idaho. And a third one in California, where he went to grad school."

His eyes widened. "All at once?"

Amy scowled, wishing she still didn't feel like such a fool for letting her romantic notions about the magic of falling in love with Ken overshadow what had really been happening. "That's the beauty of life as a winery sales rep. Apparently, you can have as many lives as you want while you travel the world."

Sympathy radiated in Teddy's eyes. He took a packet of mints from his pocket, handed her one, took another for himself. "How'd you find out?"

Another ugly tidbit. "I surprised him on a business trip to Vermont. He was staying at this very posh bed-and-breakfast, where he'd told me he also had business, but he wasn't in when I arrived. When I tried to check in as his fiancée, I was told that was impossible—his fiancée was already there. I thought it was a joke until I looked into the clerk's eyes."

"So you waited for him."

"No." Amy savored the flavor of spearmint melting on her tongue. "I told the woman at the front desk that it was all a terrible mistake, a last-ditch effort on my part to save a relationship that obviously could not be saved, and begged her not to mention it to Ken or his 'fiancée.' She seemed relieved—the last thing she wanted was some ugly domestic scene upsetting the other guests—and I left."

"Did she tell Ken after you left?"

"Apparently not, because he showed up in Laramie two weekends later, as if nothing had ever happened. I acted like nothing was wrong, too, and sent him off on a fool's errand. While he was gone, I checked out the travel logs on his laptop and read his e-mail." The guilt Amy had felt about invading Ken's privacy had been knocked out by her need to know the truth about the man she'd been planning to spend the rest of her life with. She sighed. "By the time Ken came back from town, I knew everything."

"What did he say?" Teddy demanded gruffly.

"A bunch of bull. You know… It was really me he loved. He was going to break up with the other two fiancées. He just hadn't figured out a way yet, because he didn't want to hurt their feelings."

The gleam in Teddy's eyes told Amy he knew damn well how that had gone over. "What did you say?"

"Get out. Don't call—and don't ever come back. And then I picked up the phone and clued the other two women in. Turns out Ken wasn't the guy any of us thought he was. And the worst part of it is, he's probably out there with two or three fiancées right now, doing it all over again."

Teddy studied Amy. Finally he said, "I'm not like Ken."

"I know you're not," Amy huffed. "That's why I married you."

Something inscrutable flickered in Teddy's expression. "Because I'm the opposite of Ken?"

"Yes."

"Not cover-of-*GQ* handsome and exciting?"

Amy wrinkled her nose in exasperation, irked by his baiting tone. "You're plenty handsome."

"But not exciting."

Amy opened her mouth to reply, but then didn't know what to say about that.

A determined glint in his eyes, Teddy shifted all the way toward her with a bad-boy smile that was enough to make her stomach drop. "Time we changed that, don't you think?"

The next thing Amy knew she was all the way in his arms. His mouth was lowering to hers. She barely had time to brace herself and then his lips were locked on hers in a hot, passionate kiss that took her breath away. He caught her head in his hands, and she melted against him, completely overwhelmed by the minty, masculine taste of his mouth, the unhurried pressure of his lips and the gentle stroking of his tongue. And then there was nothing but the feel of his mouth on hers. Seducing. Evoking. Commanding. Her lips parted and she sighed in contentment as he deepened the kiss even more, first sweetly and then erotically. She felt the sandpapery rub of his evening beard against her skin, inhaled the scent of man that was uniquely him, and sank deeper into the comforting warmth of his arms.

Teddy hadn't meant to kiss her this evening.

Oh, he'd known it was coming.

Living with her, being married to her, wanting a life and a child with her, had opened the door to all sorts of forbidden notions. At least in his mind. And he hadn't been the only one rethinking their decision to try to remain platonic friends while settling into their new life together. He'd known, from the way she had been looking at him when she thought he didn't see—and the way she had been avoiding being alone with him—that she was feeling the new tension between them, too.

But that knowledge was nothing compared to the experience of having her in his arms, feeling her cling to him and return his kisses with such sweet, torturous need. Amy might not be ready to acknowledge it yet, but she needed the comfort and satisfaction a real marriage could bring. She needed him. And he wanted to be there for her, he realized, as he felt her surrender to his will and surge against him. He wanted to honor and cherish her, in a way she had never been honored before. He wanted to give her all the tenderness and love she had obviously been missing. And he wanted to extract the same kind of devotion from her.

But that was going to take time, Teddy realized as her breasts flattened against his chest.

And some old-fashioned pursuing…

The kind he would have taken up had they ever actually dated.

Knowing he had to slow down or face the consequences, Teddy reluctantly broke off the kiss.

Amy looked at him with soft, misty eyes. He noted she

made no move to pull away. "What was that for?" she whispered, seeming every bit as stunned as he was by the free-flowing passion between them.

Teddy tightened his arms around her. "I'm not sure." He loved the way she felt, snuggled against him. Savoring the way her heart pounded in cadence to his, wanting to make sure this passion they were feeling was real, he cupped her face between his hands. "We better try it again."

Her breath caught in her throat as his lips touched hers. "Teddy…"

He caught her lower lip gently between his teeth. "One more time, Amy." Gathering her close once again, he gave in to the feelings stirring inside him. He kissed her long and slow, soft and deep, until she was as caught up in the all-consuming passion as he. Not about to take her for the first time in the cab of a truck, he drew back once again.

She splayed her hands across his chest, looking as if she wanted to continue making out every bit as much as he did, even while she held him deliberately at bay.

Her breath hitched in her chest. "Seriously, now…"

He grinned and stroked both his hands through the mussed strands of her hair. "Seriously," he echoed, mimicking her low tone, not about to let her confusion derail them. "There's no pretending you and I don't have physical chemistry, because it's clear we've got it in spades." And that changed everything.

Amy slumped back against the seat and covered her face with her hands. "Which maybe makes things worse than before," she lamented out loud.

Would he never understand women and what drove them? He'd felt her trembling. Knew she had been kissing him back. "I don't get it."

Her delicate brows knit together. In a low, troubled voice, she informed him, "That kind of chemistry usually goes hand in hand with romantic feelings, which—we have both agreed—we don't have for each other."

Didn't have, Teddy corrected mentally. He wasn't so certain what the situation was now. But not about to push Amy any more than he already had this evening, or go back on the word he had given her—which was that he would be satisfied with a friends-only arrangement and would never push her for anything more—he shrugged. "So maybe the only thing missing from our marriage will be romantic love," he said casually.

He'd meant to reassure Amy.

She looked more dismayed than ever. "Oh, Teddy. What happens if—instead of being okay with that—we just end up feeling worse? What then?"

Chapter Five

"Heard you had a bit of trouble yesterday," Teddy's grandfather, John McCabe, said Wednesday, when Teddy arrived to help him and his grandmother put up the outdoor decorations. Married for sixty years, the seasoned couple set the gold standard for marital happiness in the area.

"That must have been very frightening, getting stuck in that terrible weather." Lilah gently extracted the wreath from the packaging that kept it safe year-round.

"It wasn't too bad." Teddy sat on their wide front porch, untangling the string of lights that would be placed along the front-porch roof. It had been surprisingly enjoyable, sleeping in the truck, with wool blankets drawn over them and Amy cuddled up next to him for warmth. The sound of the sleet and the rain thrumming on the truck had lulled them to sleep. "The temperature rose during the night, so by dawn, it was no longer icy, just muddy. A couple of truckers came by and helped us pull Amy's truck out of the mud, and we were on our way."

"How is married life?" Lilah asked.

A glib remark was on the tip of his tongue. "Actually, I was hoping to talk to you about that," Teddy said after a moment.

"Be glad to help in any way we can," John said kindly, untangling the last of the lights.

"You two had an arranged marriage, didn't you?" Teddy knelt to plug in all the cords and make sure every strand worked. To his relief, they did.

John watched as Teddy set up the ladder at the far end of the porch roof. "It was a different time."

"We fell in love during our engagement." Lilah hung the wreath on the front door. "If we hadn't, I'm not sure I would have been able to walk down the aisle."

Teddy turned to his grandfather. "How did you feel?"

John held the lights while Teddy fastened them on the hooks. "I wanted to marry Lilah. But when we met, I wasn't nearly as romantic an individual as she was. I thought marrying a pretty woman who was kind and gentle and understanding, who wanted a family every bit as much as I did, would be enough. But then I fell in love with Lilah and I understood what she had been hoping for all along." John stepped back as Teddy climbed back down the ladder and moved it several feet to the left.

"Do you think you and Amy have made a mistake?" Lilah asked.

"No," Teddy replied, sure about this much. "I think it'll work. Amy's the one who already seems to be having second thoughts."

Lilah and John exchanged a worried look that spoke volumes.

"I want us to be a family," Teddy continued. "And I need it to happen soon." *Before Amy changes her mind and wants an annulment.* "I was hoping you might have an idea how I could make that happen."

"The first step is to act like a husband and wife." Lilah

arranged a small potted pine on either side of the front door. "Become a team."

"And you can do that," John added, "by working toward a common goal."

AMY SPENT THE REST OF Wednesday working in the greenhouse, trying to forget about the way she and Teddy had kissed each other. She was still there at eight that evening, when her husband strode in.

"If I didn't know better I'd think you were avoiding me," he drawled.

As it happened, that was exactly what she was doing. Not about to admit that to him, however, she retorted, "I'm catching up on everything that would have been done this week if Sheryl hadn't been put on bed rest."

"How's she doing?"

"Better. Her mom flew in today—earlier than Sheryl expected."

"So Ed'll be back soon, won't he?"

"Yes."

"So this could probably be done then."

Amy shrugged. "I need to get the seeds in the planting mix if I want to have starter plants to sell to the nurseries, come February."

Teddy nodded his understanding and ambled closer.

Trying not to think how handsome he looked in the suede jacket, the rim of his hat drawn low across his brow, she asked, "Did you have something you wanted to talk to me about?" *Or were you just hoping to snag a few more kisses and see where they led?*

Teddy settled on the edge of one of the heavy wooden planting tables. He stretched his long legs out in front of him and braced a hand on either side of him. "It occurred to me today when I was over helping my grandparents put the lights up on the outside of their house that you and I haven't done anything to decorate our two places for the holiday." Mischief glimmered in his eyes. "With less than three weeks to go until Christmas, that's shameful."

Yes, Amy thought, it was. Generally, she had a ton more Christmas spirit than she had this year.

Refusing to let him steer her into anything, however, she replied, "I usually just plug in this little pre-lit tabletop tree and stick a wreath on the door."

His lips curved in understanding. "Well, you're ahead of me because I've never even done that much." He reached over to trace his fingertips from her elbow to the top of the glove on her hand. "I want it to be different this year." He waited until she looked him square in the eye. "I want a tree and wreaths on the door in both places."

As much as she was loath to admit it, his was not an unreasonable request. "Okay. We'll work that in."

"And I want something else from you," Teddy continued, even more firmly. "I want you to go to the Laramie Community Hospital fertility specialist with me tomorrow afternoon."

Again, the joy she should have felt was nowhere to be found. Amy tensed, cautioning, "We're going to need an appointment."

His cheeky grin widened. "We've got one."

Amy narrowed her glance in surprise. "How'd you manage that?" she demanded.

"My grandparents helped start the hospital. I asked them to pull some strings for us, and they did."

Finished, Amy took off her gloves and set them on the table, next to the spade. "You work fast."

"Not fast enough." Teddy stood and took her hands in his.

He looked down at her so seriously that her heart fluttered. "Look, Amy, we've gotten off track. Let ourselves get distracted trying to set up the rules between us instead of focusing on the Christmas gift we want to give to each other."

She drew in a quavering breath. "A baby." His baby…

"Yes." Teddy squeezed her hands companionably. He looked down at her, like the very good friend he had always been, and heaven willing, always would. "I figure the sooner we make that wish a reality, the sooner our life together will become as happy as we both know—deep down—that it can be."

As Amy expected, it wasn't easy explaining their plan to the newest obstetrician on the Laramie Community Hospital staff.

"Let's make sure I understand," the young and personable Donna Hudson said. She sat back in her chair and ran a hand through her short dark hair. "The two of you just got married last week. You want to have a baby. And you haven't yet had intercourse."

"Nor do we plan to—which is why we want to have our baby via artificial insemination," Amy interjected, trying not to blush. Discussing such intimate subject matter in front of a member of the medical profession would have been difficult enough without Teddy sitting completely poker-faced beside her.

Dr. Hudson looked at Teddy, as if wondering if he, too, was okay with the plan.

To Amy's relief, Teddy came through for her like a champ, explaining casually, "Our marriage is based on the kind of deep, abiding love that comes out of a lifelong friendship— not romance. We both want to have a family very much."

"For a lot of reasons this seems like the right course," Amy concluded.

Apparently Dr. Hudson was satisfied they both knew what they were doing, because her manner shifted from serious to cheerful. "Well, it can certainly be done. We'll start by giving Amy a physical. Teddy, I suggest you get one from your family doc."

"Just had one two weeks ago with Amy's brother, Jeremy—he's a family doc on staff here. I'm in perfect health."

"Good. Then we'll just take care of Amy. Once the exam is complete, the nurse will set her up with an ovulation-predictor kit."

Teddy went to the waiting room, Amy to an exam room. After her physical was complete, the office lab tech came back in. She handed Dr. Hudson a slip of paper.

"Why don't you ask Teddy McCabe to come back in?" Dr. Hudson said, after perusing the note.

Unease sifted through Amy. "Is anything wrong?" she asked from her perch on the exam table.

Dr. Hudson smiled reassuringly. "Quite the contrary."

Teddy walked in, a mixture of concern and curiosity on his face. His glance slid over the pink cotton gown she was wearing and the matching sheet over her lap.

"We just tested the urine sample Amy gave us. Her luteinizing hormone has surged, which means she's ovulating. You two have a thirty-six-hour window in which to get pregnant. So if you want to go ahead and try today, I can inseminate Amy."

Joy bubbled up inside Amy.

Teddy looked equally thrilled and excited.

"Sure!" they said in unison.

"Amy, why don't you hang out here, just read a

magazine, and Teddy—you can go with the nurse." Dr. Hudson grinned at Amy. "See you in a few minutes."

Amy took a magazine from the shelf mounted on the wall and sat down to wait.

And wait.

And wait.

A half an hour went by.

Then another.

The more Amy sat there, the more nervous she became.

She wanted a baby with Teddy so much, but the circumstances were colder, more sterile, than she had expected.

Finally, the nurse came back in. "I'm sorry, Mrs. McCabe. It's not going to happen today."

"Wh-why?"

"You should ask your husband. Let him explain."

The nurse gave Amy another sympathetic look, then slipped out of the exam room.

Amy's knees trembled. She slipped off the table and began to get dressed.

Teddy was waiting for her in the reception area. His eyes gave nothing away.

She paid the bill for the visit, then walked out with him.

Their footsteps echoed on the polished linoleum flooring of the hospital annex, where the doctor's offices were located. Teddy was flushed and tight-lipped. "What happened?" Amy asked as they reached the elevator.

Teddy took her elbow and followed her into the elevator. "I don't want to talk about it."

"Well, I do!" Amy said as the doors slid shut, wrenching free of him. "What in the world happened in there?" Why had everything that had suddenly been going right suddenly gone wrong?

Teddy leaned back against the opposite wall. "I

changed my mind!" He pushed the words between clenched teeth.

Amy blinked. "About having a baby?"

Teddy gave her a droll look. "About doing it the new-fashioned way."

It took a moment for the meaning behind his words to sink in. When they did, Amy felt heat well in her chest, before moving to her neck and face. "We agreed!" she whispered, stunned and dismayed. The fact they could have a baby together without actually ever having sex with each other was the entire reason they had risked their friendship and gotten married!

His handsome jaw took on the consistency of granite. "Well, now I'm un-agreeing!"

Amy stared at him in consternation, barely able to believe they had been so close to getting what they both wanted, what would make all their mutual dreams come true, only to have him chicken out! "Teddy—for this to work…for us to have a baby—you have to do your part!" she cried, just as the elevator doors slid open. The involuntary chuckles and gaping expressions on the faces of the people waiting on the other side let Amy know the onlookers had indeed caught every word of her last sentence.

Teddy turned and glared at Amy. Reclaiming his grip on her elbow, he rushed her past the sea of shocked faces and raised eyebrows. "Nice, Amy."

She cringed and bit down on an oath. "I didn't mean to embarrass you."

He increased his strides, forcing her to struggle to keep up. "Too late. That horse already left the corral."

Amy dug in her heels. "I still don't get why…"

He pushed out the front doors of the lobby, still hurrying her along. The moment they were out of earshot of others, he wheeled on her. "You think what they asked me to do was easy?" He lowered his face till they were eye to eye. "Well, let's go back up to Dr. Hudson's office and have you go in the room and work yourself up to a fever pitch, knowing the nurse and the doctor and the office lab tech and Lord only knows who else, are all out there, waiting for you to—"

Amy lifted both hands in surrender, unable to hear more. "Okay, okay. I get the picture!"

"Do you?" Teddy straightened, six foot four inches of furious male. "Because I don't think you do—although that easily could have changed, since the nurse asked me if I wanted her to go and get you so *you* could assist me in doing what I needed to do. Should I have asked her to do that?"

Amy's face burned as much as her conscience. She stepped back a pace. "No. Heavens, no!"

Teddy braced his hands on his waist. "So we're going to have to come up with another way of accomplishing this."

Amy wrinkled her nose in confusion. "What other way is there?"

He merely looked at her.

"Oh…no…" she whispered, as the image he wanted to evoke came to mind.

Teddy put his hands on her shoulders, his touch gentle. "Amy, we have the chemistry." He looked deep into her eyes. "We proved that when we kissed the other night." He paused and tightened his grip on her persuasively. "I'm fairly certain if we were to think of this as a necessary 'procedure,' we could rally to the occasion and get into the spirit of the big event."

To Amy's shock, the idea of making love to Teddy

wasn't nearly as unnerving as it should have been. Nor was the idea that he might use the desired end result as a way to satisfy his basic male needs. Hadn't he been more open to lovemaking without traditional romantic involvement from the very first?

"There has to be another way," she insisted nervously.

His expression grim, Teddy released his hold on her and stepped back. "Well, if you think of it in the next thirty-six hours, you let me know."

THEY'D DRIVEN TO THE appointment in his truck. Hence, Amy had no choice but to accompany Teddy back to the Silverado. As soon as they arrived, she got out of his pickup truck and into hers. Without another word to him, she started the engine and drove to her ranch. She needed time alone. To think. To figure out if she could continue on with this charade of a marriage she had entered into with Teddy McCabe.

Wishing—not for the first time—that she had a big soaking tub like the one in Teddy's master bathroom, she shucked her clothes and climbed into the tiny vinyl shower stall. As the hot water sluiced down on her tense shoulders, she leaned her head against the wall and waited for the tears to come. To no avail. She could no more cry and release her deep disappointment that way, than Teddy had been able to…

Not that she could have done what was asked, either, if she had been him, Amy realized in mounting frustration.

There was something just so wrong about her and Teddy creating a baby in a doctor's exam room.

It would have been one thing had that been the only way feasible to achieve pregnancy. Then it would have been more than okay.

Had this been a real marriage and artificial insemination were required, she would have assisted Teddy. He would have been there with her, when the doctor did the medical procedure. Their baby still would have been created in an atmosphere of incredible love and tenderness. The clinical details…the presence of others…would not have mattered.

Amy ran a hand over her hollow abdomen.

Was this the way it was always going to be?

She had thirty-six hours.

And, it seemed, a mighty important decision to make.

TEDDY STOOD IN THE BARN, mulling over the irony of his situation. Two hours earlier he had been unable to perform the necessary functions at the necessary time, and now, here he was, as usual overseeing the same functions—albeit equine—that made him one of the most sought-after horse breeders in Texas.

Teddy leaned against the chute wall that separated the mare in heat from his prize stud. The two animals went nose to nose, teasing each other and getting acquainted while Mother Nature spurred them on. Knowing what was expected of him, Catastrophe allowed Teddy to lead him to the nearby breeding dummy and got down to business.

Short minutes later, the collection bottle had been filled.

Teddy praised the beautiful stallion and returned Catastrophe to his stall, then took the contents to the adjacent ranch lab for examination. Finding it good, he put the life-giving material in a syringe, returned to the waiting mare and inseminated her.

Teddy praised the mare for her cooperative attitude

and returned her to the isolation unit where she would stay until her owner picked her up at the end of the week.

Contemplating how easy the two animals made the procedure look, he returned to the lab to sterilize the equipment. If only he could take his emotions out of the process, too, and let impregnating Amy be simply a matter of biology and timing.

Instead, Teddy found himself wishing for the impossible.

Wishing they were really married. That she was his wife in more than the legal sense.

It might be out of the question but he couldn't help wishing Amy were sharing his bed, letting him indulge every fantasy that had come to mind since the moment they had said their vows.

"I thought I might find you here."

Teddy looked up from his task. "Amy."

Damn but she looked beautiful in the dim light of the barn. Her golden hair fell in soft, untamed waves to her chin. The red turtleneck sweater hugged her torso, emphasizing the slenderness of her waist and the fullness of her breasts. Her dark denim jeans molded to her waist and hips, lovingly clung to her long, sexy legs.

Teddy stripped off his gloves and walked away from the equipment he had just sterilized. "I wasn't sure you were coming back."

"I've been thinking." Amy rocked forward on the toes of her boots. She stuck her hands in the back pockets of her jeans. She tipped her chin at him, her high, sculpted cheeks glowing pink against the fairness of her complexion. "Do you think it would be possible for us to try to have a baby together again? Only this time," she finished softly, "I'd like to do it the old-fashioned way."

AMY DIDN'T KNOW WHAT Teddy's reaction was going to be. She didn't expect him to brush by her and head for the house without a word.

Whirling, she took a few quick running steps to catch up with him.

"You're not ready," he said curtly, still not looking at her.

"How can you say that?" Amy followed him in the back door.

He bypassed the kitchen and headed straight for the master bedroom.

"A few nights ago you practically wigged out because we kissed." Teddy shucked his denim jacket and pulled his shirt over his head.

Mouth dry, Amy watched him continue to disrobe.

Aware this was some kind of a test—one she was determined not to fail—she kept her eyes squarely on him as he finished disrobing and strutted toward the shower.

Damn, but he had a magnificent body, she noted through the glass enclosure. Satin skin covered taut muscle. Lower still, he was just as well…made. With difficulty, she lifted her eyes from the apex of his thighs, to his face. "That's because we were just doing it for recreational purposes," she defended herself hotly. And because it had made her feel like they were on the verge of a romance…a one-sided romance, that would have left her at a distinct disadvantage.

He arched a brow and stepped beneath the spray.

"I've had a change of heart." She'd decided she could make love without being in love after all.

Teddy regarded her skeptically.

"This time we'd be doing it for a very good reason," Amy said, continuing to make her case hurriedly, aware if she thought about it too much she'd lose her nerve. "It'd be part of our Christmas gift to each other."

Teddy shook his head in mute frustration, even as his lower body rose to the challenge. "I know you, Amy. You'll never go all the way."

Maybe she wouldn't if she didn't want a baby with him so very much. She folded her arms in front of her militantly. "I will, too!"

"Really?" Teddy turned to adjust the temperature of the spray, giving her a fine view of his backside.

"Yes, really!" Amy wished he would take her seriously.

"Then prove it." Teddy turned toward her once again, making no effort to hide his desire. His eyes locked with hers as he rubbed soap over his chest. Lower still. "Go in the bedroom. Take off your clothes. And wait for me."

Amy could see from the sardonic curve of his lips that he still didn't think she had the nerve.

She turned on her heel and marched back out of the bath. "I thought it was going to be a lot easier to be married to you!" she called over her shoulder.

"No kidding!" he called right back.

Huffing in exasperation, Amy marched over to the bed and stood staring down at it for one long second.

"This is to make a baby," she whispered to herself defiantly, already toeing off her boots. "Our baby. And he or she will be made in the spirit of tenderness and hope and love." This baby would be the ultimate Christmas gift to each other.

With trembling fingers, Amy turned back the covers.

Hearing the water shut off behind her, she closed her eyes and reached for the hem of her sweater.

"I'm not sure I understand the rationale for closing your eyes while you undress yourself."

Amy gulped again and opened her eyes.

She turned to see Teddy lounging in the doorway, his strong, tall body glistening with droplets of water, a towel draped around his waist.

"Oh, hush," she grumbled, irritated he had just spoiled her semiromantic mood. Now, she was going to have to work to get it back again.

He strode toward her, smelling of soap and man and…the potential for sex. "The fact you can't even undress without an attack of nerves should tell you you're not ready for this."

Amy let out a nervous little laugh and finished removing her sweater. "I may never be ready for this." Sex with her best friend. It didn't change the fact she wanted a baby. His baby. "Which is precisely why we should keep going."

Teddy lifted his hand to her breast, his fingertips caressing the swell of flesh above her lacy black bra.

Suddenly, he wasn't the only one getting aroused.

He regarded her ardently, a sense of purpose glittering in his eyes. "This isn't a game of Red Light, Green Light."

Amy's heart gave a nervous kick against her ribs. "I know."

His voice dropped. "If we get started…"

She let out a shuddering breath as she tilted her face up to his. "We're not going to stop."

"Exactly." Gently, he scored his thumb across her lips. "So now's the time for second thoughts…."

Defiantly, she held the challenge in his eyes. "I don't have any. Don't want any."

"Amy…"

Yearning welled up inside her. Not just for a baby now. But for him. Amy went up on tiptoe, wreathed her arms around his neck. She pressed the softness of her body against the hard length of his. "Kiss me, Teddy. Kiss me the way you did the other night."

Their lips met halfway in a fierce explosion of heat and need, want and passion. She put everything she had into the kiss, fitting her lips to his, adjusting her head to just the right angle, experimentally touching his tongue with hers. She expected gentleness, acceptance. Instead, his lips were hard and hungry, his tongue hot and wet and unbearably evocative. Taking command, he kissed her again and again, until she was lost in the taste and touch and feel of him, lost in the ragged intake of his breath and her own low, shuddering moan. And suddenly the idea of making hot, wild love with Teddy McCabe was every bit as enticing as the sight of him, clad in nothing but a towel.

Teddy hadn't expected Amy to take him up on his challenge. But now that she had…now that she was in his arms, kissing and holding him like there was no tomorrow, he could no more walk away from her than he could have not married her.

Maybe they didn't love each other in the usual head-over-heels way, Teddy reflected, dropping his towel and divesting Amy of her bra. But they did have a connection between them that was as deep and enduring as anything he had ever dreamed. Excitement building inside him, he sifted his hand through the silky texture of her hair. Her body shuddered and softened against his, and he let all he wanted come through in another deep, searing kiss. He wanted to be a husband to her in every way, and as he undressed her and drew her slowly down to the bed, she seemed to want it, too.

Sensing the need pouring out of her, he cupped the soft

weight of her breasts in his hands, bent his head, loving her with mouth and lips and hands. She clung to him wordlessly, arching her back, moving restlessly beneath him. He stretched out beside her, catching her by the waist. Shifting her onto her side, he pressed his hips against hers, kissing her again and again, until she was in a frenzy of wanting, murmuring her need low in the back of her throat. Wanting her to have everything she deserved, he made his way down her body, engaging every sense, until there was only the driving need, and the throbbing of his body and hers.

He slid upward, capturing her lips in another kiss.

"I want you," she whispered, taking him in hand.

Her breath hitched as he filled her.

Yielding to him with the sweet surrender of a woman who should have been his long before, she clasped his shoulders and trembled as he kissed her and possessed her again and again. Their bodies took up an age-old rhythm, until there was no doubting how good this felt, how good they were together, and would always be….

Teddy slid his hands beneath her, lifting her to him, driving deep. Together, they soared toward a completion more stunning and fulfilling than anything he had ever felt. More incredible for him than the feel of her beneath him, her arms and legs wrapped around him, was the thought that at this very instant…they might be making the baby they both wanted so very much.

AMY HAD NEVER BEEN A particularly sexual person, never imagined she could feel this way about the lifelong "friend" who was now her husband, but Teddy's love-making had made her feel white-hot. As if she was not just capable of conceiving the child they yearned for, but was all woman, too. As capable of giving…and receiving… emotional comfort and physical ecstasy.

"That was incredible," she whispered in Teddy's ear, wanting him to know just how wonderful he had made her feel. She could see now she shouldn't have worried about the lack of traditional romance in the making of their baby. What she had just experienced was one of the most powerful and compelling—not to mention unbearably tender—moments of her entire life.

Teddy chuckled, pressing his lips against her neck in a series of hot kisses. "Tell me about it!"

Still shuddering with reaction, she rested her head on his shoulder. She liked the unexpectedly sexy turn their relationship had taken as much as the sound of his low, husky voice. With a sigh of contentment, she splayed both hands across his chest. "Who knew?"

He found her lips with his. His kiss was tender and sweetly coaxing. "I guess we should have."

Aware that she had waited a lifetime to feel like this, Amy searched his eyes, needing somehow to put a label on this, so that it wouldn't all ease away, as quickly and unexpectedly, as it had occurred. "What does this mean?" Were they married now—in their hearts? Or was this the friends-with-benefits scenario he had once proposed?

Teddy smiled and gave her a lazy once-over, seeming every bit as contented as she now felt. "It means," he said, gently disengaging their bodies and rolling so that she was on top of him, "that we're every bit as compatible—in a marital sense—as we first thought."

Not exactly the declaration of undying love she had hoped to hear. Amy lamented softly, "Except that so far we fight about everything."

Teddy stroked a hand down her spine, eliciting tingles

of delight that made her want him all over again. His slow smile was as enticing as his touch. "Maybe not making love is what we've really been fighting about."

She tensed as his manhood pressed against her inner thighs, hot and hard. "You think?"

He shrugged, making no effort to hide the fact that he wanted to make love with her again every bit as much as she wanted to tenderly explore him. "I feel a lot more at peace with things now." He tunneled his hands through her hair and captured her bare lips with his. "How about you?"

Amy let him shift her onto her back once again. "Definitely."

"There's only one problem." He draped one leg over hers.

"What?" Amy'd never felt so warm and safe. Never believed anyone could desire her with such ferocity.

Teddy smiled, his eyes glowing with a determined sensual light. "I don't know if I'm ever going to want to get out of bed again."

Chapter Six

It seemed to Amy that she and Teddy had just gotten to sleep after their night of marathon baby-making, when the alarm beeped. With a groan, Teddy shut it off.

Amy struggled to sit up, saw it was six o'clock.

Teddy pressed a kiss on her bare shoulder, ran a caressing hand down her spine. "You should try to get some more sleep if you can."

"I wish I could." Amy yawned, not sure when she had felt that well-loved. Every inch of her tingled with the memory of his touch. Wrapping her arms around her legs, she rested her face on her upraised knees. She watched appreciatively as Teddy stretched, rubbed the sleep from his eyes and reluctantly rolled out of bed.

He picked up the clothes he'd left on the floor and carried them into the bathroom, where he put them on top of the overstuffed hamper.

Amy stood and pulled on a robe. She picked a brush up off the bureau and ran it through her hair. "But I've got to get going, too."

Teddy set the full hamper next to the hall door, for transport to the laundry room, then went back to his closet where only a few pairs of jeans and two clean canvas work shirts remained.

"Getting down to the wire there, aren't you, cowboy?" Amy teased.

Teddy grinned at her. "I've got a couple days left before I have to do laundry."

"Like to wait till the very last minute, do you?"

He shrugged his broad shoulders. "That way I only have to do it once a month."

"It must take all day."

"Pretty much. But then I don't have to worry about it. Let me guess. You're a laundry-once-a-week kind of gal."

"More like two or three times a week. I only like to do a load or two at a time, at most. And that includes my delicates, which have to be washed separately."

She could see the mess in the laundry room—and the overflowing hamper in the master bath—was going to bother her, in the long run. Fortunately it was nothing that had to be dealt with today. Amy didn't want anything ruining the glow she felt, after a night of ardent lovemaking.

Oblivious to her thoughts, Teddy headed for the bathroom. "Where do you want to sleep tonight?" he asked, running a razor over his morning beard.

That, at least, was easy. Amy squeezed toothpaste onto her brush. "Here."

His eyes met hers in the mirror. Clearly stunned by her newly cooperative attitude, he said, "Again?"

Amy shrugged as she rinsed and wiped her mouth on a towel. "How about from now on?" She rubbed liquid complexion soap over her face. "It really doesn't make sense for you to try to fold yourself into my much smaller bed."

He caught her against him and ran a finger down the foamy white cream on her cheek. "It might be fun if you were in there with me."

"I want you to be comfortable," Amy said. She

wanted them to be able to make love unencumbered. There was no way Teddy and she could do that crammed in a trailer bedroom that was barely bigger than the double bed it contained.

"I want you to be at ease, too," Teddy murmured.

Pulling her to him, he used his free hand to dampen a washcloth and remove the soap from her face. Finished, he dipped his head and found her lips with his. Amy tingled all over as they indulged in a long, steamy kiss. She knew they were just friends, but if this wasn't romantic, she didn't know what was.

Slowly, Teddy lifted his head and he gazed down at her with desire. She knew how he felt. When they'd married, she hadn't expected such thrilling passion, either.

He flashed a crooked grin and traced the side of his hand down her face. "I better go before I'm tempted to stay and make love with you all over again."

Amy turned her head and kissed the center of his palm. She knew he was right. They could easily pick this up later, when they had all the time in the world….

"Are you going to the marathon cleaning and painting session of the chapel this evening?" she asked.

He nodded.

Amy smiled, glad to be working with him on something so important, not just to the community, but to themselves. "Then I'll meet you there."

It was only after she had spoken that Amy realized how cozy and domestic their morning "routine" had been, and how very much she suddenly felt like Teddy's wife.

"You look gorgeous tonight," Susie told Amy, hours later.

Broom and dustpan in hand, Amy's sister Rebecca

joined them in the center of the chapel. "You're positively glowing," she concurred.

If so, it was a warmth that came from the inside out, Amy thought. She pushed the trash can across the stone chapel floor, assisting in the pickup of the debris left over from the storm and resulting fire.

On either side of the chapel, volunteers were busy removing damaged sections of drywall and wooden pews that needed to be either replaced or refurbished.

"We weren't sure what to expect…." Susie scooped up bits of tree, leaves and burned roof.

Rebecca made a face. "We heard about the scene in the hospital lobby—or was it elevator—yesterday afternoon."

Amy paused to admire the new sections of drywall going up. With a fine new roof overhead, the chapel was going to look like new in no time. "That's the beauty of working out on my ranch most of the time." She made a face right back. "I miss all the gossip."

Rebecca swept another square clean. "You don't seem worse for wear. Maybe this marriage is a good thing."

Amy knew it was. But it was also so new and precious she didn't want to share her feelings with anyone just yet.

She changed the subject. "How are the twins?"

Rebecca exuded the excitement of a new mom. "Wonderful. Exhausting. Perfect. Sweet." She chuckled. "They're also up all night, every night. We've got both their grandmothers taking care of them this evening, but they're both so busy with their own careers… I don't know how Trevor and I are ever going to get any Christmas shopping done."

Up until now, Amy had been avoiding spending too much time with the twins. She knew it was selfish, but being around babies had made her lament her own lack of children too much. Now that she and Teddy were married and actively trying to have a baby, she no longer felt that way. In fact, she was eager to make up for lost time. "Teddy and I could babysit for you, if you two want to go out some evening."

Rebecca perked up. "Could you do it Friday?"

"I'll have to check with Teddy, but I think he's pretty flexible. In any case, I can do it."

One of the volunteers set up a boom box. Christmas music filled the sanctuary, adding to the festive mood.

"You two still trying to have a baby?" Susie asked, obviously referencing the scene at the hospital the day before. "'Cause if you are, I've heard being around babies helps stimulate all those maternal hormones and feelings."

"Susie!" Rebecca chided.

"It's true." Susie chuckled. "Haven't you heard how people who've never been able to conceive, adopt a child, and then boom—they're pregnant?"

"I don't think Amy's situation is the same," Rebecca said, glaring at the four months pregnant Susie.

"Well, whatever her situation is, I've never seen her looking happier," Susie commented. She leaned close. "What is going on with you two, anyway?"

Amy flushed.

"Are you and Teddy…?" Susie persisted.

In love? The unspoken words hung in the air. Amy wanted to say no, out of habit, but she knew that wasn't true any longer. Not after last night. The truth was their passionate lovemaking had shown her a side of Teddy that she hadn't ever allowed herself to see. He was hot. She wanted him. She *might* even be falling in love with him. And he with her…?

Susie's jaw dropped open. "Oh, my gosh." She looked at Rebecca, still in total shock. "I think they're…"

"Stop!" Amy held up a hand. "You both need to slow down with your observations and assumptions." They all did. The last thing Amy wanted was her romantic desires to ruin what she and Teddy had. "Teddy and I are taking it one step at a time." It was the only prudent thing to do. "If I look happy tonight it's because it is finally beginning to feel like Christmas to me."

The best Christmas, in fact, that Amy had ever had.

TEDDY HAD BARELY CLEARED HIS pickup truck when his triplet brothers, Trevor and Tyler, approached.

"We need to talk."

Given a couple of the text messages he had been receiving throughout the day, Teddy had an idea what this was about. "No, we don't." Anxious to see Amy after a day spent apart, he strode toward the chapel doors—only to be cut off by Amy's brother, Jeremy.

"Yeah, I think we do," Jeremy said.

Teddy exhaled and stopped where he was in the parking lot.

"We all heard what happened yesterday at the hospital," Trevor said, as if he were the authority on marital relations, just because he had been the first of the triplets to tie the knot.

"We're not sure what part of the baby-making process you are having trouble with," Tyler added, with a smidgen of the soothing manner he used as a large-animal vet.

"But in any case—" Jeremy reached into the inside pocket of his blazer and withdrew a white envelope "—I brought you the handout I give the patients in my medical practice on how to optimize the chances of getting pregnant."

"Assuming you've got the basics down pat," Trevor teased, with a knowing wink.

"If you need help with those…" Tyler added, chuckling.

"Well, at your age…" Jeremy shook his head as if it were a lost cause, if that was the case.

Teddy shot them all a droll look. "Very funny, guys."

"Seriously, stress is not good for making babies," Trevor said.

"You want success, you've got to be all romantic," Tyler added.

Jeremy nodded, with a physician's sage attitude. "Show her that you really care."

Teddy held up a hand. "You guys don't need to worry."

Trevor scoffed. "That scene yesterday says otherwise."

"Amy and I worked it all out," Teddy countered.

Three sets of male eyebrows raised.

"And that's all I'm going to say," Teddy added firmly, folding up the handout and putting it in the back pocket of his jeans.

There was a long, skeptical silence.

Then three slow grins.

The light of recognition in their eyes.

Trevor was the first to slap him on the back. "If this means what I think it means—that you and Amy are in a real marriage—way to go!"

"Congratulations, dude!" Tyler shook his hand.

Jeremy nodded his approval. "I've always said Amy needed to stop being so frivolously romantic and go for the real thing. Apparently, she's found it."

"Thanks, guys," Teddy said. He only hoped he and Amy didn't lose what they had found the previous night. Their success in the baby-making department had been so unexpected. Amy could be skittish, especially when she was feeling overemotional. He looked all three men straight in the eye. "I really want this to work out." And for the first time since he and Amy had said their vows, he felt like they had a chance.

"WHAT WERE YOU AND JEREMY and your brothers talking about in the parking lot?" Amy asked when they got home.

Teddy took in the anxious look on Amy's face. "How'd you hear about that?" he asked, hanging up their coats. More important, what had she heard? He didn't want her upset or embarrassed in any way. To that end, he was prepared to do whatever had to be done.

"I went out to see if you had arrived yet, and I saw them laughing and smiling and slapping you on the back. It seemed like a guys-only kind of moment, so I went back inside. And then I got drafted to wash the soot off the stained-glass windows, so I got caught up in that."

Teddy knelt to light the fire he'd built in the hearth.

"So back to my question about what was going on out there…?"

"Oh, yeah. Our brothers. They're all happy we're married and going to have a family. Naturally, they were full of 'advice' on how to achieve that."

Amy looked like she wanted to sink through the floor. "You didn't tell them…we…"

"C'mon, Amy," Teddy countered gruffly. "You know me better than that. I've never been one to kiss and tell." Although, their brothers had all quickly surmised as much, he recalled ruefully.

"But…" he reached into his back pocket, glad for the opportunity to move the conversation along, to something much more important to both of them. "Jeremy did give me a copy of the handout he gives his family-practice patients who are trying to have a baby."

Amy cast a look at the laundry room, where clothes took up every available inch of floor. With a slight frown, she closed the door, then went to the fridge and opened it up. "What does it say?"

Teddy scanned the suggestions. "We should both be drinking our milk and having tea instead of coffee. We're not supposed to be imbibing alcohol. I'm supposed to be wearing boxer shorts. We should be making love every one to two days, at least during the window of opportunity."

Smiling, Amy poured two glasses of milk and unwrapped the plate of gingerbread cookies. "I think we covered that last night."

Teddy grinned. "So we did." He munched on a cookie and kept reading. "Uh-oh."

"What?" Amy paused, mid-sip.

"We're supposed to be using the missionary position."

"We did."

"The first time." The second time they had been a little more adventurous.

"Do you want to try again tonight?"

Amy looked so hopeful that Teddy suddenly feared her disappointment if they didn't conceive this month. Willing to do anything to give her what she most wanted for Christmas—their baby—he referred to the list of instructions once again and told her practically, "It says here sperm count is higher in the morning than at night. Since this is the end of the window of opportunity…what do you think?" He paused, reading her expression. "Should we wait until morning?"

IT WAS A VALID QUESTION. Thoughtfully posed. Yet Amy felt as if she had been punched in the stomach. All the blossoming romantic feelings—and Christmas spirit— that she had been experiencing, abruptly faded. To be replaced by uncertainty and doubt.

"Sure." Amy finished the last of her milk in a single gulp and turned away. "I'm a little tired tonight, anyway."

Teddy came up behind her and put his hands on her shoulders. "We can make love tonight if you want." Still holding her gently, he turned her to face him. The warmth of his hands transmitted through her clothing to her skin.

"What does the handout say?" Seeing a streak of soot on his chin, she reached up and wiped it away. "Is there a problem if we make love too many times in a certain period?"

She could see he didn't want to answer.

Aware she needed to know, she arched a brow and waited.

He frowned and admitted reluctantly, "With some men, yes, the information did say that too-frequent lovemaking can reduce the sperm count, but it's not the case in all men."

Amy bit her lip, torn between momentary pleasure and their long-range goals. She looked deep into his eyes. "But it could be the case with you."

He shrugged.

"Then morning it is." Amy pushed aside her disappointment and tried not to think how much she had been longing for this very moment—when they were alone and could make love again. Morning was just hours away, after all. She'd waited years to have a baby.

In the meantime, she needed to ask him something. "I hope you don't mind, but I told Rebecca that you and I would babysit for the twins Friday evening so she and Trevor could go Christmas shopping."

Reaching for another cookie, Teddy grinned. "Sounds fun."

Amy felt compelled to warn, "She said the twins are a handful right now."

Unperturbed, Teddy drained his glass. He took her by the hand and led her toward the fireplace. "Most four-month-old babies are, from what I've heard."

"Are you up for it?" Amy settled on the sectional sofa beside him.

"Are you kidding?" Teddy pulled her into the curve of his arm. He pressed a kiss on the top of her head. "It will be good practice for us."

FOR A SECOND, TEDDY THOUGHT he had made a mistake, putting the science of procreation ahead of the emotional considerations of making love to his new wife. But as they continued to talk and enjoy the evening, Amy relaxed. By the time they hit the showers and went to bed, she was all too willing to let him pull her into his arms and give her a long, leisurely good-night kiss.

Exhausted, content in a way he hadn't been in a very long time—if ever—Teddy fell immediately into a deep sleep. When the alarm went off hours later, Amy was no longer in his arms. Rather, she was stretched out along-side the edge of the opposite side of the bed.

While he rubbed the sleep from his eyes, she rose gracefully and disappeared into the bathroom. He heard water running, the sounds of her brushing her teeth. Figuring it wasn't a bad idea to do the same, he waited until she came back, then got up.

When he returned to the bed, Amy was lying on her back, waiting for him, the covers drawn to her collarbone.

The pale pink T-shirt and pajama pants already on the floor let him know she wasn't wasting any time.

He couldn't fault her for that. Even though they'd allowed a good hour or hour and a half for the pleasurable "task" ahead of them, there was no sense in wasting precious moments struggling to get out of clothing they weren't going to need, anyway.

He let his boxers fall to the floor, then lifted the edge of the covers and climbed in beside her. "Good morning, Mrs. McCabe."

"Good morning," Amy replied in a voice tight with tension.

Figuring he knew exactly how to relax her, Teddy took her into his arms and began kissing her bare shoulders, the nape of her neck, the shell of her ear, her cheek. As he had expected, Amy's breath quickened. Her body heated.

Still, he took his time finding her lips with his. Even longer delving into her mouth.

Amy murmured a sound that should have been acquiescence, but wasn't. She returned his kiss, but instead of the sweet, sure passion of the other night, the exchange was awkward, out of sync.

Figuring maybe they just needed time to wake up, Teddy rolled so he was on his side, bringing her with him via the pressure of his arm on her waist. Flattening his palm on her spine, he brought her closer still. Or tried to—when his hand dipped to the small of her back, instead of curving into him, letting hardness meet softness in that fundamental man-woman way, Amy tensed even more, and drew back slightly.

Teddy tried again, by cupping her breast, but felt her withdraw.

He exhaled, broke off the not-so-great kiss and lifted his head. "What's wrong?" he asked softly.

Amy pressed her lips together and wiped the moisture in her eyes away with the back of her hand. She barely met his eyes before dropping her gaze once again. "Nothing."

"Don't you like to make love in the morning?" He ran a caressing hand down her bare arm, from shoulder to wrist. "Is that it?"

Teeth raking across her lower lip, she shook her head in mute denial, then sat up, dragging the blankets with her. "It's... I don't know. I can't seem to get in the mood, but I know we should do this so I want you to just go ahead." She gulped in more air and lay back down.

It was his turn to sit up, only he made no effort to cover himself with the sheet. The ache in his loins was still there, but he could feel his spirits deflating like a leaky balloon. "Amy, I want to have a baby, too, but not unless you're in the mood."

"I'm trying." Sudden tears trembled on her lashes. "Please." She held out her arms to him. "Let's just do it."

Teddy lay back down beside her. Once again, he gave it his all. Once again it didn't seem to make a damn bit of difference.

"DON'T YOU LOOK LIKE YOU'VE lost your best friend," Ed said when he walked into the Laurel Valley Ranch greenhouse, several hours later.

No kidding, Amy thought.

Her and Teddy's planned morning lovemaking session couldn't have been more of a disaster had the bed collapsed beneath them.

She never had been able to relax.

Teddy had been concerned, hurt and frustrated.

In the end, they'd given up and promised they'd do it

again later, just in case the window of opportunity was still the slightest bit open. But Amy wasn't kidding herself....

Until last night, when she had seen Teddy with that list of instructions her physician brother had given him, she'd thought—hoped—that something magical and romantic was happening between them. She'd imagined he was falling in love with her every bit as much as she was falling in love with him.

Only to discover it was all about having a family, after all.

Given how much she wanted a child, that should have delighted her.

It didn't.

Instead, she felt foolish and hurt and emotionally exposed in a way she had never been before.

She'd let herself go with Teddy, in a way she had never done before. And it had been more than just the physical. She had completely opened her heart to him. Let herself think they were starting a new chapter in their life together, one that had all the traditional romantic elements of a strong and solid marriage. Only to find out it was all about friendship and having a baby together in the most efficient way.

And now...now she had to figure out how to leapfrog back to where they had been before they'd made love that first time, to the place in her heart where she didn't expect or want quite so much, the place where she would be able to settle for what her husband was able to give her.

"Earth to Amy...earth to Amy..."

Amy looked up, realizing her employee had been talking to her for several minutes and she hadn't heard a word of it.

She put down her spade and gave Ed her full attention. "I'm sorry. What did you say?"

"We've rescheduled the couple's baby shower for a week from Saturday. Obviously, we can't have it at the restaurant now, with Sheryl on bed rest, so we're going to have it at the house. I assumed you would want to bring Teddy, now that you're married." The words were casual, but there was a question mark in his eyes.

Amy figured Ed was wondering the same thing as everyone else. Was this hasty marriage of hers going to last?

Yesterday morning, Amy had been certain of it.

Now she didn't know what was going to happen, over time.

Ed carefully moved starter plants to bigger pots. "Do you want to issue the invitation? Or shall I?"

"I'll ask him." Amy flashed a confident smile she couldn't begin to feel. "We promised Rebecca and Trevor we'd babysit the twins tonight. I'll do it then."

Chapter Seven

Rebecca and Teddy were both running late when they met up at the Silverado that evening.

Because he only had one full bath in his ranch house—albeit a very luxurious one—and time was running short, they were forced to share quarters as they got ready to go over to Rebecca and Trevor's. It seemed to him that the close proximity was apparently a lot harder on him than it was on her. Seeing her wrapped in a robe, knowing she was fresh out of the shower and had on nothing but her birthday suit beneath the thick terrycloth, had him aching like there was no tomorrow.

Stripped down to his boxers, he hid the proof of his need for her by turning into the bathroom sink.

While he shaved, Amy stood in front of the sink at the other end of the long bathroom cabinet and ran a comb through her damp, fragrant-smelling hair. "I hope tonight goes okay," she said.

Teddy watched as she put a small dab of some sort of hair product in her palm and sensually worked it through her hair, from root to ends.

Trying not to recall how those same hands had felt, gently caressing him, he focused on his task and spread shaving cream over his face. "You're the last person I'd expect to be apprehensive about babysitting."

Amy flashed him a wry smile. "I know we can handle the mechanics of taking care of the babies." She switched the hair dryer on low and began running warm air over her damp honey-blond hair, the lighter streaks around her face turning platinum as they dried. "It's just, up to now, seeing the twins has been bittersweet for me." Amy paused to meet his eyes in the mirror. A mixture of emotions glittered in her soft eyes. "I'm hoping it will be different now that I'm married and going to have a baby of my very own."

My very own.

Not *our* very own.

Trevor pushed aside his disappointment. One day soon she'd be thinking of the baby they were trying to conceive as theirs. Taking in the unbridled hope shining in her eyes, knowing how deeply romantic she was—and how easily she could get disappointed—he felt compelled to caution gently, "It may not happen the first time out of the gate, you know."

Amy tensed, as if she didn't even want to consider the possibility that they might have to try to conceive again and again before they got the desired results. She shrugged and turned away from him. "Then we'll keep trying," she said tensely.

But what if it didn't happen for months? Teddy wondered. He stroked the razor across his face, shaving away the day's growth of beard. Would Amy become discouraged if it took six months or a year or more? Lose interest in marriage and him?

Misunderstanding, Amy turned off her hair dryer and came close enough to touch his arm. "My lack of…enthusiasm…this morning was a mistake that is not going to happen again, Trevor. I'll get into it next time, I promise."

Teddy knew it wasn't that simple. Men were more straightforward in their wants and needs. Desire in a woman was a complicated thing. And that was especially true with a romantic like Amy.

Giving him no chance to comment further, she slipped out of the bathroom, shutting the door behind her. Glad for the privacy, Teddy stepped into the shower and turned the dial from warm to cold.

When he emerged, Amy was on her cell phone with her sister Susie, taking an order for more landscape plants. They continued talking business during the drive over to the Primrose ranch house, where Rebecca and Trevor had been living since they were married. Trevor's house was right next door, on the Wind Creek, but Rebecca and Trevor had opted to reside at Rebecca's home, since it was bigger and more family-friendly.

"Jenny and Joshua are sleeping in their cradles in the family room," Trevor said as he ushered them inside. "Rebecca's writing out the list of phone numbers."

"And what a long list it is," Amy laughed, allowing Teddy to help her with her coat.

Rebecca made a face at her younger sister. She handed the legal pad of numbers over. "Give me a break. I'm a new mom and you never know who you might need to call. The pediatrician, fire department."

"I know we know our own parents' phone numbers," Teddy said, perusing the list.

Rebecca made a face at him. "In an emergency, people sometimes can't recall what they need on the spot."

Trevor motioned for Teddy. "Come in the kitchen. I'll show you how the bottle warmer works."

"I've also written down what time they should have their next bottle. Although all times are approximate since we feed on demand." Rebecca wrung her hands. "Obviously, they'll need diaper changes throughout the evening. I've written down when those are most likely to occur."

Amy touched Rebecca's arm. "Take a deep breath. It's okay. There's two of them and two of us. We're not going to be outnumbered. Furthermore, Jeremy is right next door. And although our brother can be very annoying at times, especially when he's waxing on and on about that broken-down ranch he purchased and can't yet live in, he's also a fine family physician. Should a medical emergency occur tonight he will be here in thirty seconds flat."

Trevor reemerged, holding Rebecca's coat and what looked like another long list. "If we want to get our Christmas shopping done tonight, hon, we need to get a move on."

Rebecca started to launch into another long list of instructions.

Trevor clamped his hand over his wife's mouth and playfully compelled her out of the room as if she were a vaudeville comedian who needed to exit the stage before a riot ensued. "The stores are open late. So don't expect us back before midnight. Food and beverages are in the fridge, so help yourselves. And stay away from the mistletoe!"

"Cute," Teddy quipped.

Trevor grinned as if he knew it.

Rebecca rolled her eyes and they left.

Alone at last, peace stole over them. "What should we do?" Amy asked eventually.

Teddy took Amy's hand and drew her toward the sofa. "I suggest we relax while we can."

"Good thinking."

Amy turned her attention to the sparkling lights on the evergreen in front of the window. "Their Christmas tree is beautiful."

Teddy nodded in agreement. Aware how much more of a family home this was than either his or Amy's place, he murmured, "We really should get ours up. Rev up the yuletide spirit."

Amy reached over and took his hand. Her fingers felt small and delicate in his. "The stockings on the mantel are sweet, too."

Teddy nodded his agreement. "It really feels like Christmas here."

"I like what they've done with their photographs, too."

Teddy turned his eyes to the collection of sterling-silver frames on the end table. One captured Trevor and Rebecca at the party officially announcing their engagement. Another showcased a professional pose from their wedding. The next was a snapshot of Rebecca in late pregnancy, Trevor's hand on her belly. And, of course, there were photos of the four of them in the hospital, after Jenny and Joshua's birth.

The wistful look in Amy's eyes as she studied the family photos said it all. Too late, Teddy realized just how much he had taken from Amy, marrying her the way he had.

Jenny stirred.

Amy released her grip on Teddy's hand and got up to take a peek at the babies. "They're waking, Teddy. We better get those bottles warmed and ready…."

SEEING TEDDY WITH THE TWINS made Amy realize how much she wanted to have a baby with him. The four-month-old babies adored him, too, cooing and smiling up at him while he paced back and forth with a baby cradled in each arm.

Finally, diapers were changed, bottles were warmed and they were all set. Amy settled into a rocking chair with Joshua, while Teddy sat down with Jenny.

Contentment permeated the cozy room. And along with it, the fear that things might not work as wonderfully for her and Teddy as they had for Tyler and Susie…and Rebecca and Trevor.

What if she couldn't get pregnant right away? What if it never happened? Or she had a baby, and Teddy realized it was the child he really wanted—not a life with her—after all?

"I know what you're thinking," Teddy said.

Nerves jumping, Amy pushed the unsettling thoughts away. "You do?"

"Sure. You're wondering why your two sisters get all the romance—and you don't. Fortunately, there's an easy fix for that." Teddy looked up from the infant in his arms and flashed a smile at Amy. "All you have to do is go on a date with me tomorrow night."

Amy stared at Teddy in confusion. Even when they were just friends, he'd always been able to read her too well. "Aren't we past that stage of our relationship?"

Teddy tilted his head. "How can we be past it when we've never been there?"

Amy shifted the baby in her arms to a more comfortable position and drew a stabilizing breath. "But we're married, Teddy."

Deliberately, he held her gaze. "Married people have date nights. My parents always did."

"So did mine, but our relationship isn't the same as

theirs." Legend had it that both sets of parents had been madly in love when they tied the knot. She and Teddy— sadly—weren't. And odds were, never would be. Not in that all-encompassing way.

His lips took on a rueful curve. "Exactly why we have to go."

Amy couldn't deny the notion of embarking on a traditionally romantic outing with him held a surprisingly tantalizing appeal. Was this the start of something better? "Where do you want to go?" She forced herself to sound casual.

Teddy waggled his eyebrows. "That's for me to know and you to find out."

Noting Joshua was drifting off to sleep again, Amy set the bottle aside and wiped a bubble of milk from his mouth with the corner of the burp cloth. She sat the baby up to burp him. "I have to know what we're going to be doing so I'll know how to dress."

Teddy shifted Jenny to his shoulder. "Wear something warm and comfortable and not too nice," he advised Amy, while patting the baby's back.

Amy lifted a brow. What did *not too nice* mean? And what did that say about his plans?

"Like jeans," Teddy clarified.

Amy pursed her lips. "What if I want to wear cashmere?" she teased him right back.

Teddy winced. "Not really a good idea. Although I would wear a hat and gloves. But not a scarf…unless you want to tuck it into the neck of your coat. Then it'd be all right."

"Okay. Now I'm curious," Amy said as Joshua let out a resounding burp that had them chuckling.

"Yeah, well, you know what they say about curiosity,"

Teddy chided. "It's no help to a person unless they're planning to be a detective."

Amy gave him a dirty look.

Teddy frowned as Jenny began to squirm and fuss. "What's wrong here?"

"Just a guess, but it looks like Jenny wants to burp. Here. You take Joshua and I'll take Jenny."

"This is better," Teddy crowed as Joshua settled right down to take the rest of his bottle.

Amy sat Jenny up on her lap. One hand supporting her tummy, she used the other to pat her back.

Jenny kicked her arms and legs and looked all the more uncomfortable. Not to be outdone by her brother, she burped, too. Albeit not as loudly.

As Amy settled Jenny in her arms again and began giving her the rest of the bottle, she caught Teddy watching. She knew he wasn't in love with her, but the expression on his face was so tender, so completely enamored, it had her heart skipping a beat.

Before she could let herself get carried away with romantic notions, Amy turned her attention back to the baby in her arms. "Back to date night," she drawled.

Teddy offered a sexy half smile. "I like the sound of that."

Amy forced herself to concentrate on the practical side of what was happening between her and Teddy, not what she wished would happen. "If you choose this week," she cautioned stubbornly, "next week I get to choose what we do."

Teddy's glance roved her slowly. He appeared to be contemplating all sorts of things, the least of which was making love with her again. "What are you going to choose?"

Amy flushed. "I'm not telling!"

He nodded as if to say "Aha!" "A woman of mystery. Hmm. I like that."

Amy liked the new turn in their relationship.

Aware Jenny looked ready to sleep again, Amy carried her over to the changing pad on the sofa, put on a fresh diaper and swaddled her in a receiving blanket before laying her down in the cradle. Teddy brought Joshua over and did the same, before settling him in his cradle, too.

They stood there a moment, side by side, making sure the babies were nodding off, then slipped into the kitchen to finish their conversation. "You realize you're flirting with me?"

He took her hand in his, letting her know with a look and a touch that they had nothing to be nervous about. "You realize you're flirting back," he murmured.

"Flirting wasn't part of the bargain."

"Maybe it should have been." Tightening his fingers over hers, he drew her closer. "Now, where was that mistletoe we weren't supposed to stand under?"

"Teddy!"

"Ah…here it is…." A mischievous look on his face, he backed her up to the doorway of the family room.

"We're babysitting," Amy protested breathlessly.

Wrapping an arm around her waist, he pulled her close enough to feel the heat and tension in his tall frame. "The babies are asleep."

Feeling his immediate arousal, as well as her own tingling response as their bodies rubbed up against each other, Amy pushed playfully at his chest. "Sitters are not supposed to kiss their boyfriends when they are on the job…."

His tempting smile widened. "Good thing I'm your

husband, then," he whispered, taking her chin gently in his hand, lowering his head to hers. She murmured a sound of protest as their lips connected. "Teddy…"

He brought his other hand up and threaded it through her hair. He pressed a kiss to the corner of her lips, her cheek, her temple. "Just another kiss, Amy. Just one." He stroked the shell of her ear with his tongue. "That's all I ask." He fit his lips over hers. "We'll save the rest for later."

The caution protecting Amy's heart disappeared. Sweet surrender rippled through her. She met his passion with her own. Feelings swept through her, intense and true. She poured them all into the kiss. And of course that was when the front door opened and Rebecca and Trevor walked in.

The shock on her sister's face morphed swiftly into delight. "You two are romantically involved!" Rebecca said, her arms full of bags.

Trevor, on the other hand, did not look at all surprised to find them making out.

Flushing, Amy disengaged herself from Teddy's warm embrace. "More like married and trying to get into the Christmas spirit by indulging in a harmless kiss beneath the mistletoe," Amy said, as if it were the most unemotional thing in the world to be doing.

"Married *and* trying to have a baby together," Rebecca quipped, looking both happy and worried for Amy. "Although the last I heard *that* was supposed to be done the artificial insemination way."

"That's old news," Trevor corrected his wife with an affectionate chuckle. Looking at Amy's face, Trevor amended hastily, "Or maybe not."

TEDDY TRIED TO MAKE CONVERSATION several times on the drive back to his ranch. Amy responded politely, but her heart wasn't in it. Because he wanted to look into her eyes while they talked, he waited until they walked into the ranch house before calling her on the sudden shift in her mood. "Look, I don't know what's going on, but I can see that you're upset—"

"With good reason, it would appear. What exactly have you been telling people about our love life?"

Teddy noted she had said love life, not sex life. That was a plus. "Nothing."

Amy's lips firmed. "Obviously something, or your brother wouldn't have said what he did."

Teddy grimaced. "Our nuptials created shock waves throughout the community. Everyone is curious. Everybody I run into wants to know how we're adjusting to married life."

"And?"

"I tell them we're doing great."

Her delicate brow arched. "So it's important to you what people think."

Teddy wished it wasn't. But being the biological son of a man who hadn't thought twice about divorcing his wife and giving over sole custody of his triplet sons gave a guy issues when it came to his character. Teddy had always worked overtime to make sure he was as unlike his biological father—and like Travis, his adopted father—as possible.

Teddy didn't just coexist with others. He went out of his way to lend a helping hand whenever possible. He made sure he was friendly and cheerful in his dealings with everyone.

Right now, Amy was putting his easygoing attitude to the test. "Of course it matters what people think." He wanted to be known as a good guy. He wanted his family and friends to be proud of him. "Doesn't it matter to you?"

She ignored his question. "So it would help your rep in the community if people thought there was something romantic—rather than simply friendship-oriented—going on between us."

"There is!"

Amy scowled, her frustration with the situation apparent. "One night of lovemaking for the sake of procreation, and shared babysitting and a little flirtation does not a romance make! Okay—" embarrassed, she rushed on before he could interrupt "—so that wasn't as articulate as I would have liked. You know what I mean!"

He hung his coat up next to hers on the coat tree next to the door. "What I see is you making a big deal out of nothing."

She whirled on him, her silky hair flying out to brush his chin. "You think I'm wrong to be upset with you?"

He stared down at her, just as mulishly. "Damn right I do!"

Temper flared in her dark-brown eyes. "You know, initially I would've felt bad about putting you out of your bed. Not anymore." She aimed a finger his way. "You're sleeping on the sofa!"

Teddy scoffed. "Darlin', you can't lock me out of our bedroom."

Her smile only tightened. "Oh, really, cowboy? Watch and see!"

Teddy stood there weighing his options after she threw a blanket and pillow at him and slammed the door in his face. Part of him wanted to do the movie-hero thing and kick the door in, take her in his arms and kiss her until neither could recall what they were fighting about. And while the hopelessly romantic side of Amy might appreciate that as much as the privately romantic side of him, the practical side of Teddy knew it would be a mistake. You didn't school a horse with attitude and overwhelming force. And you didn't woo a woman that way, either.

You achieved rapport with cool reason, understanding and patience.

Like it or not, if he wanted to make this situation work, he was just going to have to bide his time.

Chapter Eight

"Thanks for the prompt delivery." Susie signed off on the order of potted pine trees, suitable for post-holiday planting, and poinsettias. "I've really had a run on Christmas items this week. And it being Saturday, I expect even more customers today." She paused. "Everything okay with you?"

Unable to keep her feelings in check any longer, Amy exploded, "What is it about men—and marriage?"

"Care to elaborate?"

Amy slammed the doors shut on her delivery truck and walked up the loading ramp, to Susie's side. "They're one person before they get a ring on their finger, and then voilà, they become someone else entirely."

Susie motioned for one of her high school employees to come and get the last of the shipment, then took Amy's arm and steered her into her private office at the back of the store. "They often say the same thing about us women."

Susie filled a cup with water and slid it into the microwave. "Have you ever known Teddy to be a braggart?"

"No. Even when he has reason, he usually doesn't tout his accomplishments." Amy ripped off her gloves and coat and slumped into one of the side chairs next to Susie's desk. "Yet he has no problem going all over town and telling everyone what a hot sex life we have."

Susie smiled and rummaged through a basket of tea bags. "Did he actually say that?"

"He may as well have." Amy scowled. Heat rose from her throat to her face. "Everyone thinks we're…?"

Susie made a "keep it coming" motion with her hand.

"…sleeping together," Amy finally finished.

Susie shrugged. "You *are* married."

Amy ignored the ding of the microwave. She watched Susie remove the cup of steaming liquid and drop a tea bag into it. Instantly, the room was filled with the scent of chamomile. "It's no one's business whether we're having sex or not."

Susie added a squirt of honey and stirred it with a spoon. "Are you?"

"I'm not telling you."

Susie looked triumphant. "You are."

Amy's cheeks flushed all the more. Embarrassed, she turned her glance to the file cabinets. "That's not the point."

"It's precisely the point." Susie pressed the cup of soothing tea into Amy's hands, and got a small bottle of milk out of the minifridge for herself. "You two have only been married a couple of weeks, and already you've gone from 'just friends' to…"

"…friends with benefits." Amy figured she might as well say it out loud. She had to talk to someone. Try to get some perspective here.

Susie smiled. "Well, that's good, isn't it? It should make things a lot easier in so many ways. You'll be able to have a satisfying sex life as well as a best friend, and kids you're both going to adore. What's not to like about that?"

Amy took a long sip of tea in an effort to calm herself. She looked into her sister's compassion-filled eyes and confided, "It's just gotten so confusing, Susie. When Teddy and I went into this marriage, it was all very clear-cut. We were friends. We were going to the doctor's office to conceive. Everything was going to be just the way it was before we tied the knot except we'd have a family of our own."

Susie perched on the edge of her desk. Like most newly expectant mothers, she had that special glow, that near-perpetual state of excitement. "And now it's not that simple," she empathized.

"No. It's not," Amy agreed. The change was making her want more out of the relationship, it was making her want things that might not even be possible between them—and she knew that wasn't fair to either of them. Teddy had always been very clear how he'd felt about her: she was a pal. Not someone he was interested in romantically, despite what he was currently leading people to think, for the sake of both their reputations around town.

Susie studied her carefully. "What else is bothering you?"

"Teddy is making assumptions he never would have made before."

"Give me an example."

"He made dinner at my place without asking me, in my kitchen, and made a horrible mess in my oven."

"He didn't clean it up?"

Amy threw up a hand in exasperation. "Of course he did. The point is he never would have invaded my personal space that way before we were married. At the very least he would have asked first. And he would never have discussed our relationship with anyone else."

"Forgive me for interrupting, but aren't we doing the same thing?"

Amy flinched. "You know what I mean."

"Yes, I do, and I hate to say it, but I think this is all bull. What's really gotten you so out of sorts this morning?" Susie narrowed her eyes. "Did something happen last night when you were babysitting at Rebecca and Trevor's?"

Amy rubbed her fingers down the front of her jeans. "We had a stupid fight when we got home. I got completely overemotional in a way I don't usually do, and told him he had to sleep on the couch."

"And?" Susie probed.

"And," Amy recollected miserably, "he did."

"Looks like the twins' christening will be held here— on the twenty-third—after all," Travis McCabe said, Saturday afternoon.

Teddy surveyed the interior of the community chapel. A crew of forty men had been busy since early that morning. Wiring and plumbing had been repaired, new drywall put up, paint applied and stained-glass windows cleaned. A new organ and bell for the tower had yet to be installed, the landscaping outside redone, pews brought in, but with a sturdy roof overhead and the interior nearly finished, the chapel stood as a beacon of hope and faith in the center of Laramie once again.

Teddy smiled at his dad. "Amazing what pulling together can accomplish."

Travis loaded scrap drywall and finishing tape into a wheelbarrow. "Speaking of teamwork...how's the marriage going?"

Teddy knew he could evade the question and his dad would let the subject drop. He didn't want to do that—he needed some fatherly advice. Teddy finished picking up the scraps and turned the wheelbarrow toward the exit. As soon as they were out of earshot of others, he confided, "Going from being just friends to husband and wife is a lot more complicated than I expected."

"And yet, nearly two weeks later," Travis observed, "you're still hanging in there."

"I want it to work." Teddy loaded the scraps into the bed of his pickup truck, for transport to the dump. "Were you and Mom friends before you started dating?"

Travis reached into the cab and brought out two plastic water bottles. He handed one to Teddy. "We became friends while I was pursuing her. That doesn't mean it can't work the other way around."

Intrigued, Teddy waited for him to continue.

"You want my advice?" Travis asked as the December sun warmed their shoulders.

"If I didn't, I wouldn't be asking." Teddy uncapped the bottle and took a long sip.

"Forget trying to have a baby for the moment. Slow down. Let that kind of intimacy unfold gradually and naturally. As old-fashioned as it sounds, it seems to me you owe Amy a lot more wooing than she's had."

Teddy thought about his father's advice. There was no doubt Amy was a traditional woman, at heart. She was not the kind of gal who would hook up with any guy on a whim. Yet that was exactly what he'd been asking her to do. No wonder she was ticked off at him for going about their quest for a baby in such a practical, matter-of-fact way.

She might say she was okay being friends-with-benefits, as well as potential life mates and co-parents, but what she really wanted was a little more romance in her life.

Teddy had promised her, at the outset of their marriage, that "love" would not be expected or mentioned. He was a man of his word. He would honor that promise. But he could still give her everything else she had ever wanted and needed. He could make her feel like the very desirable woman she was. He could concentrate on having fun with her, instead of trying to establish their rules or marking out their turf.

Most important of all, he could make their first Christmas as husband and wife a holiday they would always remember. Starting right now.

MINDFUL OF THE TIME, TEDDY hit a restaurant and bakery before he left town, then went home to shower off the drywall dust and change. From there, he drove the short distance to Amy's ranch.

At four o'clock, Teddy walked into Amy's trailer, his heart in his throat.

As agreed—before their very first fight as a married couple—she was waiting for him to take her out on their "date."

"Ready to go?" he asked, aware of the short amount of daylight they had left.

With a cranberry scarf laced about her neck and clad in a thick white sweater, jeans and boots, Amy looked delectably feminine—and surprisingly vulnerable.

Hands propped on her hips, she studied him skeptically. "You still want to do this?"

"What do you think?" Teddy took her in his arms and did what he should have done the previous evening. He kissed her, until the stiffness fled from her limbs and she melted against him. Before long, all the anger, emotion and lingering resentment between them morphed into something warm, sweet and welcoming.

He lifted his head. "I'm sorry."

Amy splayed her hands across his chest. "No. I'm sorry." Tenderness mixed with the apology in her dark-brown eyes. "I behaved ridiculously last night."

He tucked a lock of pale-blond hair behind her ear. "We both did."

Her arms circled his neck. She went up on tiptoe, her manner soft and earnest. "I don't want to fight with you," she whispered.

Teddy tunneled both his hands through her hair. "I don't want to fight with you, either," he said gruffly.

They kissed again. Deeply, more irrevocably this time.

She looked up at him with misty eyes. There was nothing he wanted more than to carry her to the bedroom at the other end of the cozy abode and make hot, tender love to her, but if he did that, the rest of his plans would be dashed...and they were too important to ignore.

"We better get going." He exhaled, reluctantly backing away from her. Taking her by the hand, he led her toward the door. "We don't have all that much daylight left."

"Why do we need daylight?" Pulling on her jacket, she followed him down the trailer steps.

Teddy studied the color in her cheeks. "It helps to be able to see when you're picking out a Christmas tree."

Her brows lifted in surprise. "We're doing that tonight?"

"About time we put one up at the Silverado ranch house, don't you think?" Teddy picked up the small tree saw he'd left by the door. He waited for her to fall into step beside him, then headed for the fields where she grew hers.

Amy pulled on her gloves. "Teddy, I sold all the bigger ones. The pine trees I have left are only three or four feet high."

Teddy transferred the tree saw to his other hand and wrapped his arm about her waist. "It's not the size of the Christmas tree that counts, it's the emotion you feel when you pick it out, and our first tree has to be a Laurel Valley Ranch Christmas tree. Nothing else will do. I want our first official holiday as husband and wife to be a Christmas to remember," he said softly. "I want to start a tradition of going out every year and picking out a tree together and then putting it up and decorating it. I want our kids to look forward to it every year as much as we do."

Two hours later, they fit the tree they'd selected into a tree stand and considered where to put it.

Teddy didn't need to be a genius to see Amy was displeased with the result of their efforts. "Obviously, you're thinking something," he drawled, wishing just this once she wasn't such a perfectionist when it came to plants.

Amy folded her arms in front of her. "You want me to be blunt?"

"Always," he fibbed, bracing himself for the worst.

"It looks even sillier than I thought it would."

Teddy turned his attention to the four-foot Virginia pine tree with short needles and dense foliage. "So it's not that tall." And now that they had it inside, the branches were definitely a little thicker on one side. "It smells great."

Amy's frown deepened as she walked around, surveying the room and the tree from all angles. "Everything in this room, from the cathedral ceiling to the sectional sofa, fireplace and plasma TV, is man-size." She tapped one of the branches. "I'm not sure this even qualifies as kiddie-size."

She had a point about that. He hadn't taken scale into consideration when deciding where to get their tree. "It'll be fine once we get it decorated." Teddy set it a safe distance away from the hearth. And if she still was unhappy, they'd move it over to her trailer, where it would look huge, and have their Christmas there….

Amy regarded him with a look of barely checked skepticism. "This may be one time, cowboy, when your optimism is misplaced."

Figuring the sooner they got lights on the Virginia pine tree they'd cut down, the better, Teddy picked up one of two cardboard boxes they'd picked up from the storage shed at her ranch.

"Furthermore, I'm not even sure what's in those boxes."

"It says *ornaments* right here." He pointed to a corner of the box, then whipped out his Swiss Army knife he carried in his pocket for just such occasions.

"Yes, but what kind?" Amy fretted, giving him a reproachful gaze. "I've been collecting decorations for years."

"So?" Teddy put the knife away and ripped off the excess package tape, before wadding it into a ball and tossing it aside.

"My taste hasn't always been very adult." Determined not to let him see, she tried to elbow him aside.

Curious, he got there first, anyway. He pulled out a shoe box nestled in all the tissue paper, took off the lid, and blinked. "I didn't know they made cartoon figure ornaments."

She scoffed. "You're kidding, right?"

He shrugged. "I never actually shopped for any." Truth be told, he'd never had his own tree. Never gone to any effort to make a Christmas for himself and the women in his life. And whether she was ready to admit it or not, Amy was his, had been since the very first time they'd made love.

"We don't have to use these." Amy put the lid back on the box and set it aside.

Teddy shrugged, not sure what the big deal was with women and decorating. "They looked fine to me."

Determination drew her brows together. "There's got to be something better in there." Amy pulled out a box of velvet bows and red wooden beads strung together to look like strands of cranberries. "This might do."

Teddy certainly hoped so. He was getting hungry, and Amy'd already indicated on the ride over that she didn't want to eat dinner until they'd finished their task.

He opened up the second box marked Indoor Lights. "Multicolored or white?"

Amy bit her lip as she considered. "Not sure yet."

This was going to take forever, he moaned inwardly. "Then how about both?"

She made a face.

He made one back. "It's our tree. We can decorate it any way we like." Noting the sudden stealth of her movements, Teddy paused. "What's that?"

Amy tried to put the unopened package of ornaments back in the tissue paper before he could see it clearly. Not about to be thwarted, Teddy plucked it back out. "Baby's First Christmas Tree Ornament Set," he read.

Amy flushed with obvious embarrassment. "I bought it a couple of years ago, thinking just having this ready to go might change my luck."

"And obviously they have," Teddy interjected. "You are married now. Actively trying to have a baby with me." As the pink in her cheeks deepened, with a different kind of awareness now, Teddy started to open the top. "We should put them on the tree."

Amy shook her head and covered his hand with her own. "I don't want to jinx it."

Teddy looked into her eyes and realized how deeply disappointed his wife was going to be if she didn't conceive right away.

Maybe she was right.

Maybe it was best to wait on the baby ornaments.

Hoping she wouldn't suffer that kind of discouragement, he handed the set back. She put them back in the box and pulled out yet another shoe box marked Texas. Recognition lit her dark-brown eyes. "I forgot I had these, too." Beaming, Amy said, "I think we've got this year's theme!"

"Admit it," Teddy said as the two of them finished their supper, side by side, on the sofa. "It's a really beautiful tree."

Amy admired their handiwork. The pine tree was still small, but it had a Texas-size appeal. Strands of red, blue and white minilights lit up the branches. Miniature red, blue and white bandannas, shiny silver stars and golden lassoes adorned the tree. The quilted tree skirt featured a Western-garbed Santa, and a sleigh full of gifts, pulled by eight longhorns.

Amy smiled. "I do like it." A lot more than she had ever expected.

Teddy stacked their dinner plates and headed for the kitchen. A few minutes later he returned with two pieces of chocolate pecan pie, heaped with big scoops of vanilla-bean ice cream.

He waited until she had claimed her dessert, then settled beside her. "And to think it only took us three hours," he noted with a satisfied smile.

"Four and a half if you include the time it took to chop it down and drag it back here." Amy let the rich confection melt on her tongue.

"Worth it?"

She nodded. "It feels more like Christmas already."

Teddy studied the room. "We still need stockings for the mantel."

"That's easy enough to manage," Amy said. "I'll borrow my mom's sewing machine tomorrow when I pick up the book of baby shower games she's lending me."

"I meant to tell you. I got invited to that, too."

"Planning to go?"

"Wouldn't miss it. Although I'm not sure what to do about a gift for that or the twins' christening." He paused. "You want to go in together?"

Acutely aware that wasn't a question most married couples would have to ask each other, Amy said, "Sure."

Mischief lit his eyes. "Want to be in charge of picking 'em out?"

That did sound like a husband. At least, the ones she knew. "Be glad to."

"You let me know what I owe you?"

Amy nodded.

"Did you get enough to eat?"

"Too much." All she wanted to do was take a nap.

"I forgot the coffee." Teddy grabbed their plates and took off. "I'll be right back," he called over his shoulder.

Amy stifled a yawn and settled deeper into the cushions of the sofa. "Take your time."

The next thing she knew she was being slowly lowered—onto Teddy's king-size bed. Amy moaned. She must have fallen asleep. "Oh…no…"

"Shhh!" Teddy said, slipping off her shoes and covering

her with the comforter. "Go back to sleep." He kissed her brow, then moved off again.

Chagrined at the way their first date was ending, Amy tried to wake up all the way, but the forces pulling her back into sleep were too strong.

When she woke again, it was barely dawn.

Teddy was fully dressed, walking out the bedroom door with a duffel bag in his hands.

Alarmed, Amy pushed up on her elbows and gave him a questioning look.

He came back to her side, sat on the edge of the bed. Freshly showered and shaved, he was dressed in a dark-blue corduroy shirt and jeans and smelled as good as he looked. "I forgot to tell you I had to leave on a business trip today, didn't I?" he asked softly.

He certainly had. Disappointment filtered through her. "When will you be back?" Amy pretended an ease she couldn't begin to feel.

Teddy gestured vaguely. "If I'm lucky—Wednesday evening. I have to deliver a couple of foals in different parts of the state—they're early Christmas presents—and then pick up two brood mares and stop by and talk to a couple of other prospective clients about breeding one of my stallions to their mares. I'll try to call you, check in, from time to time. But a lot of it, as you know, depends on weather this time of year. On the Oklahoma and New Mexico borders road conditions can get wicked, fast."

Amy nodded.

Teddy wrapped his arms around her and pulled her close. He gave her a deeply romantic goodbye kiss that was a gift in and of itself.

"When I come back," he vowed in a low, husky tone,

"you and I are going to finish that date night the way it should have been finished."

Amy's pulse raced. She returned his flirtatious tone. "And how is that?"

He smiled with a promise that had her insides heating. He pressed another kiss in her hair. "Guess you'll just have to wait and see."

Chapter Nine

"Where's Dad?" Amy asked her mother Sunday afternoon. As always, the kitchen smelled delicious this time of year, like fresh-baked confections and mulled apple cider. She paused to ladle herself a mug of the steaming brew from the pot on the counter.

Meg looked up from the gingerbread house she was decorating. "There are fresh-baked spritz cookies in the tin, if you'd like some. And your father is over at the chapel, helping move in the new pews."

Amy frowned, disappointed. She had come to think of the restoration of the chapel as her personal undertaking, aligning the progress being made there with the positive "rebuilding" changes in her own life. "I could've helped with that." Would have if she had known the replacement pews that had been ordered were ready for installation.

Meg scooped more thick white icing into the pastry bag. "No ladies allowed today. Too much heavy lifting. You are on the schedule, however, for the holiday decorating of the chapel on Wednesday evening." Her smile broadened. "Teddy can come, too."

Amy hesitated. "I'm not sure if he'll be back by then." Finding her mother's cookies too good to resist, she pried off the top of the tin and helped herself to a handful of the small, star-shaped butter cookies. "He's on a business trip. Which is why I came over to borrow your sewing machine." Amy pulled up a stool to the kitchen island and sat opposite Meg. It didn't seem to matter how old she got— hanging out in the kitchen with her mom always made her feel happy and content. "I'm going to make play quilts for the twins, as christening gifts, and stockings for our mantel."

"That sounds fun." Meg fit a different nozzle on the end of the bag and piped icing along the roof line. She studied Amy with a mother's keen eye, as if wondering what the status of Amy's marriage was.

Amy would like to know that herself....

It wasn't as if she could have gone with Teddy on his trip, when she was already shorthanded and had so much work of her own to get done.

Still, it would have been nice to be asked.... Nicer still to know he regretted having to be away from her as much as she was already regretting being away from him.

"Did you need any material?" Meg asked helpfully, mistaking the reason behind the slight frown that had crossed Amy's face.

Amy shook her head and pushed away the desolate thoughts. "I stopped at the fabric store before I came over here."

Meg motioned for Amy to have a seat. "As long as you're here you can help me with some of these gumdrops...."

Amy grinned. "So long as I get to eat a few."

"Not too many," Meg chided, with a cautioning lift of her brow.

She went back to icing the other half of the roof. "So how are things going otherwise?"

Amy sorted the candy by color, feeling some questions she'd prefer not to answer coming on. "What do you mean?" She feigned nonchalance.

Meg lifted her slender shoulder in an elegant shrug, then probed Amy with yet another compassionate gaze. "You seem a little glum."

Amy sighed. Leave it to her mother to be able to read her like a book.

"Does this have anything to do with Teddy being away?"

Amy concentrated on placing gumdrops in a perfectly straight row. Even before she spoke, she could feel herself getting defensive. "You know I'm used to being on my own."

"Which makes your reaction to his absence all the more curious," Meg noted gently, then went over to get a mug of mulled cider for herself. She leaned against the counter, taking a break. "Unless it's something else that is bothering you?"

Amy needed some female wisdom, regarding relationships and marriage. Her mother could provide that, and would do so without judgment. "For as long as I can remember, Teddy and I have been completely in sync with each other," she said finally. "It's what made us feel that turning our long-standing friendship and shared values into a marriage was going to be a cinch."

"And now?" Meg asked gently.

Amy sat back and shook her head. "I feel like we're doing this dance. Only I don't know what the moves are anymore. I'm trying to follow his lead. He's trying just as hard to intuit what I need. But we keep tripping each other up."

To the point she'd fallen asleep during their first actual date!

Amy rubbed her finger on a smudge of icing on the

island, back and forth, until it almost disappeared. "The funny thing is that I don't feel single anymore, but—" Amy paused and bit her lip as she looked her mother in the eye "—I'm not sure I feel married, either."

And she really wanted to *feel* married. Not just have this ring on her finger and McCabe as a last name.

Amy drew a deep breath. "I guess what I'm asking is how do I go from being Teddy's friend to his wife?"

Meg's eyes darkened. "You act like one."

AMY LUGGED THE PORTABLE sewing machine and the sack from the fabric store into the Silverado ranch house, her mother's advice still ringing in her ears. To Meg and probably every other woman in Laramie, the solution to Amy's problems was iron clad.

If you wanted to be married, you had to act married.

But how was she supposed to do that, when Teddy was as deeply entrenched in his own way of doing things as she was? His approach to laundry, Amy thought, being the perfect example.

She'd noted when he had left that morning he had taken the last of his clean clothes from his closet and dresser drawers. Which meant when he came back he wouldn't have anything clean to wear. Not a pair of jeans or shirt or socks or underwear.

Meanwhile, the laundry room off the kitchen and the hamper in the bathroom were overflowing with filthy clothing.

Amy had kept quiet about his method of wardrobe maintenance because she didn't want anyone telling her how to do things, either. But this was absolutely ridiculous, she thought as she waded through the mess to the perfectly fine washing machine.

No self-respecting wife would ever let her husband's clothing get in such a mess. If she were responsible for doing the family laundry, that was.

Teddy hadn't asked her to do this, of course.

But since when did a husband or wife have to ask their spouse for help, in order to get it? Wasn't the key to a successful marriage the manner in which the husband and wife helped, supported and loved each other, no matter what?

Maybe she and Teddy weren't in love. At least not yet, Amy amended. But they could certainly be there for each other. Starting now.

AMY WAS INSIDE THE RANCH house when Teddy pulled into the driveway at dinnertime on Wednesday. One of his part-time employees was waiting, to unload the two brood mares he'd brought back with him and get them settled in the stables. Teddy paused only long enough to give a few extra instructions and head for the house. Amy's spirits rose. Teddy had called two or three times every day he had been away. And though those discussions had been nice, it was nothing compared to the feeling of seeing him stride toward the house, his duffel bag slung over one shoulder.

Not wanting to appear too anxious, she retreated to the kitchen and hovered over the stove where a hearty beef stew was simmering.

"Something sure smells good," Teddy said, coming through the ranch house door.

Amy smiled.

He came toward her, looking like he wanted to wrap her in a big bear hug and kiss her. Instead, he set his bag down and paused, his expression shifting into one that was much more low-key. "Homemade bread, too." He nodded at the golden loaf cooling on the counter.

"And a salad in the fridge, as well."

He glanced past her, at the laundry room, and blinked.

"I did a little laundry while you were gone," Amy said.

His brows rose in silent question.

"Actually, all of it," she said.

He continued staring at her, perplexed.

Embarrassed and worried she might have overstepped, she lifted her shoulders in a nonchalant shrug. "I noticed you didn't have anything clean left. And since I was here, anyway, doing some sewing and the monthly paperwork for Laurel Valley…"

Teddy walked past her into the laundry room.

She followed as far as the doorway, watching as his eyes touched on the laundry detergent and fabric softener sitting on the shelf above the washer. He appeared to be thinking something. What, she couldn't tell. "You ran out of whatever you had," she rambled on uneasily, feeling like a girlfriend who had moved all her personal-hygiene stuff into the unsuspecting—and unwelcoming—guy's bathroom cabinet, "so I just brought over what I had." She paused to take a breath and back up a step. "It's a mountain mist fragrance. It's not too girly or anything."

The inscrutable expression in his eyes faded. He turned and strolled back to her side, still seeming upset. And trying to hide it.

He flashed the kind of polite smile he usually gave people he didn't know all that well. "That was really nice of you, Amy," he said kindly, abruptly shifting into a tone that seemed much more sincere and a lot less off-putting. "You didn't have to do all this, but…it was really nice."

It was good he thought so.

Because if he thought she had overstepped her bounds with cleaning his dirty clothes, he was really going to be ticked off at her for accepting an invitation for the two of them without consulting him first.

"Now for the bad part." It was her turn to plaster on a gracious smile. "I've got to be at the community chapel in an hour to help decorate the interior of the church. And I can't be late because I'm bringing fresh holly branches and evergreen boughs from my nursery."

Teddy clapped a hand on her shoulder, his touch far more casual than she wished.

"Give me ten minutes to shower and dress." He increased the pressure of his hand once more before releasing her. "Then we'll eat and head on out."

Still feeling a little bewildered by his strange reaction, Amy nodded and stuck her hands in the back pockets of her jeans. "Great."

Teddy retrieved his duffel bag and headed toward the master bedroom.

While he cleaned up, Amy dressed the salad with buttermilk dressing and put salad into bowls, certain something about what she had done had displeased Teddy in some way, but not really sure what.

Was it having dinner ready when he walked in? Being here, waiting? Practically with bated breath? Doing his laundry? It had to be one of those three things because he had started acting strangely even before she'd told him she had taken it upon herself to make plans for the two of them for the evening.

Whatever it was, he gave no clue as he strolled back into the kitchen, minutes later, freshly showered and shaved. He held her chair for her when she went to sit down—something else she had only seen him do with women he was dating.

During dinner, he told her about his trip, the horses he

had delivered and the reactions of the owners, the brood mares he had picked up, and the somewhat problematic meeting he'd had with yet another potential client.

As Amy listened to him, she wondered if this was what the future held. All she knew was that she liked the intimacy of sharing a meal with him at day's end, the feeling she was no longer without a husband of her very own. And hopefully soon would have a baby of her own, too.

"It feels great to be home again," Teddy remarked as they headed out to her pickup truck for the drive into town, travel mugs of coffee in hand.

"Even though you weren't actually at the ranch very long," Amy teased. Knowing he liked to drive, she handed him the ignition keys.

He shot a glance at the greenery peeking out of the tarp over the truck bed, then turned back to her with a slow, seductive smile. Arm around her shoulder, he brought her close, delivered a soft and tender kiss to the top of her head. "It doesn't matter where I am," he murmured, giving her another brief, familial squeeze, before ever so reluctantly releasing her. "When I'm with you, I feel good."

"Same here," Amy said candidly. More than she had ever dreamed possible. Which was why she had to rein in her feelings, keep her guard up. And not cross any more lines between the two of them. Teddy had made it perfectly clear to her what he expected of this union of theirs—a friend to go through life with, a loving mother to his children. And that was all. Falling in love with him was not part of the equation, so she needed to put even the possibility of it out of her mind once and for all.

Teddy wanted to live an ordinary life, without a lot of big ups and downs. He wasn't interested in infatuation, or intense emotions that would fade. He wanted to go straight to the kind of serene love people who had been married for years and years had, the kind that seemed as much—if not more—about friendship and companionship and shared family than anything else. That was what she had promised she would give him when they had agreed to marry each other. Much as she might long to explore other options, she could not—would not—do that, if it meant risking all that they had.

TEDDY KNEW HE HAD BLOWN IT, reacting as he had, when he had arrived home that evening. He couldn't help it. All he had wanted to do when he walked in was pick up where they had left off when they last saw each other. Resume their first-ever "date night," and then end it the way it should have ended, with him taking her in his arms, carrying her back to the bedroom and making wild, passionate love to her. Instead, he had walked into a cozy, old-fashioned domestic scene that seemed more reminiscent of marriages from his parents' generation, than their own. And that was really odd. Amy—like her sisters and brother—had always done everything her own way, no matter what anyone else thought or expected.

The Amy who insisted on driving the twenty-four-foot cargo truck to Wichita Falls in iffy weather all by herself, to deliver two hundred Christmas trees; the Amy who had started her own business and lived in a trailer so she could expand her nursery rather than use the profits to build herself a more comfortable ranch house; the Amy who insisted they could have their baby the scientific way without it affecting their decades-long friendship in any way. *That* was the Amy he knew…not this June Cleaver wannabe who'd apparently taken her place.

And yet, he couldn't deny, once he had gotten used to the idea of her doing all that she had to welcome him home, that her sweet domesticity was a certain turn-on, too.

His married brothers had talked about how great it was to come home to a warm and loving woman at the end of the day. They'd said being married had made them feel more—not less—of a man than ever before.

Teddy was beginning to get that.

Even as he knew he had some ground to make up, for his shocked reaction to her efforts. All he had to do was look at her face to see that her guard was up again, her inner caution light had switched on. If he wanted to be close to her again, and he did, he had to find a way to get those barriers down again.

Figuring they had to start the conversation somewhere, he picked up his travel coffee mug and shot her a curious glance. "Which use for a ranch do you think is better?" He struggled to get the drinking slot open with one hand, while he continued steering with the other. "Growing plants or raising horses?"

With a frown, Amy reached over and opened the lid so he could drink.

Teddy murmured his thanks and took a sip.

"A nursery, of course," she said, as if the argument began and ended there.

Loving the sparkle that came into her dark-brown eyes when she matched wits with him, he drew her in with a triumphant "You can't ride a begonia."

She returned his smile. "Can't ride a pregnant brood mare, either."

"Ah, but you can ride a stallion."

Amy kicked back in her seat. She propped one ankle

across the opposite knee, wiggling the toe of her boot back and forth. "I thought strenuous exercise diminished a male's fertility. Or is it the other way around?" She sipped coffee and regarded him over the hard black plastic rim of her travel mug. "You're not supposed to let go of any sperm if you want to be at your peak in other areas."

He chuckled at the superstition honored—unnecessarily, he thought—by many pro athletes. "On the contrary. Horses need to stay fit to breed. The 'if you don't use it you lose it' theory of living, as it were."

She regarded him with mock seriousness and folded her arms in front of her. "You've spoken to Catastrophe about this, have you?"

Teddy warmed to the notion that she held as much affection for the beautiful quarter horse he and his brother Tyler had rescued as he did. Tyler had used his skills as a vet to heal Catastrophe from his previous owner's mistreatment, and Teddy had given the spirited animal a home and a new purpose in life. "Catastrophe and I converse about a lot of things," Teddy drawled, trying not to notice the way her posture plumped up her breasts beneath her brown suede jacket.

Amy snickered and continued to flirt with Teddy the same way she had when they were just friends. She tugged on the ends of the white chenille scarf around her neck. "Such as?"

"The mystery of women." He waggled his brows at Amy impishly. "How to make them happy. Stuff like that."

"And what is the great stallion's advice?" she asked dryly, with an exasperated shake of her tousled blond hair.

"He tells me lightning doesn't strike twice," Teddy said softly. When they reached a stop sign at the edge of the town, he paused and gazed into her eyes. "When it's right, it's right." *The way it is with you and me.*

He instantly wished he could take those words back. Had they not promised each other they wouldn't bring love—or even the mention of it—into their relationship? The fact was they had vowed to maintain their friendship with each other at all costs, not make demands that might make either of them frustrated or uncomfortable. And he knew better than anyone that Amy mistrusted romantic love. It had taken her several years to recover after that bigamist had broken her heart and crushed her spirit. Now that she had recovered, now that she was married to him, he had to keep his word to her and not do anything that might muck up their relationship or screw up the family they were trying to have. At least not any more than he already inadvertently had.

And the first thing on the agenda was getting through the evening without any further missteps on his part.

Fortunately, by the time they reached the chapel, it looked as if the volunteer session was in full swing.

Teddy helped Amy and a host of volunteers—many who were their family members—carry the greenery that would soon be fashioned into decorative garlands and wreaths, into the chapel.

He returned to her pickup truck to find Amy nowhere in sight.

A quick glance around the exterior helped him locate her.

She was standing where the old oak tree had once been, reverently looking at the new shrubbery and the sturdy sapling that had been planted in its place.

Not sure if she was satisfied with what she saw or not, Teddy closed the distance between them. "This tree from Laurel Valley?" he asked.

Inside the church, a brass quintet and organist were

rehearsing for the Christmas services to be held there the following week. Music resonated through the stained-glass windows, lending a festive air to the wintry Texas evening.

Amy spared him a glance, then turned back to studying the young maple tree and the artistically arranged plants and shrubbery around it with a thoughtful eye. "Yes. I supplied the plants. Susie did the design and her landscape crew did the planting."

Teddy stepped closer and laced an arm around Amy's shoulder. "They did a nice job."

"I think so." Amy relaxed and turned toward him, tipping her face up to his. And suddenly Teddy could hold back no longer. He knew he had promised himself he'd go slow, give their relationship more room to develop physically within the confines of their marriage, but his feelings for her were stronger than his common sense.

Catching the look in his eyes, Amy released a shuddering breath. Stepped back. "We really should go inside," she said.

Teddy sensed she needed a hello kiss as much as he did. He was a fool for not having done it earlier. "Not," Teddy corrected softly, "before I do this."

He wrapped both his arms around her waist.

"Teddy…" Amy murmured, splaying both hands across his chest.

He had an idea what she was going to say. "I don't care who sees us," he told her gruffly, sliding his hands beneath her jacket, to her spine, and lowering his lips to hers. He covered her mouth in the midst of a sigh, and the feel of her breath in his mouth only added to the quiet intimacy of the moment. The brass quintet and organ continued to play. The beauty of the music and the crisp December air wrapped around them, while the feel of their bodies, pressed so warmly up against each other, drew them in.

She was everything he had ever wanted. He knew it now. She was everything he had ever needed.

Maybe this marriage of theirs hadn't started out the traditional way, but it was working on so many levels. Physically, they couldn't be more compatible; intellectually, they still had that ability to get each other; and emotionally…well, emotionally they were getting closer with every passing day.

To the point he could hardly imagine life without her.

A baby…if…when…it were to happen would simply be the finishing touch on an already great life together.

Amy hadn't meant to let him kiss her, not when she was feeling so needy and vulnerable. But the moment his arms were around her, the moment he pulled her close, there was simply no drawing away. She wanted to feel the pressure of his lips moving over hers. She wanted to taste the mixture of mint and coffee on his tongue. Feel the subtle stroking of lips and hands, lower still, the hard maleness that let her know just how much he wanted her.

Teddy made her feel so womanly, so hot and soft all over.

He made her realize there was so much more to life than she had ever known.

"AND I THOUGHT THE DAYS OF US making out behind the chapel were long gone," Susie teased, a good fifteen minutes later.

Rebecca looked superior in the way only a kick-butt Carrigan woman, married to a McCabe, could. She continued tying evergreen branches to a garland-length strand of florist wire. "I never did that."

Susie started laughing, as intent as ever on living her life to the fullest. "Then it's about time." Susie slanted a mischievous look at Amy. "Ask our baby sis how much fun it is misbehavin' upon occasion if you don't believe me."

This time both of them laughed.

Amy tugged on a pair of gardening gloves. She glared at her sisters. Then hissed, "Stop it, you two! Before someone else overhears." The last thing she needed was either her or Teddy's parents getting wind of this. They already thought she and Teddy had lost their minds. This kind of teenage PDA would confirm it.

Susie shrugged. "I guess we could talk about something else."

"Please." Amy wrapped holly cuttings around a wire wreath mold.

"What are you and Teddy getting each other for Christmas?" Rebecca asked curiously.

Amy swore inwardly at the oversight, which was yet another indication of just how bad she was at this whole married business, especially since she'd never forgotten to get Teddy a gift when they were just friends. "Uh…"

Her sisters chuckled. "Good answer," Rebecca drawled.

Amy tried—without much success—to keep the heat of embarrassment from her face. "What are you giving Trevor?"

Rebecca beamed. "A night in a five-star hotel in Dallas. Mom and Dad are babysitting."

Susie finished one garland and started on another. "You ought to see the lingerie she bought for the big event. I was with her when she got it."

"Hey," Rebecca chided, laughing. "I wasn't the only

one standing at the cash register. And you've planned a night he'll never forget for the two of you, too, so…"

Susie blushed.

Glad the conversation had moved away from her, Amy relaxed slightly.

Rebecca gave Susie an understanding look, then turned back to Amy and went on conversationally, "The one thing I never knew about pregnancy was how completely hot it makes you. I mean—" her voice dropped to a hush "—you want to have sex all the time."

"Rebecca, please! We're in a church!" Susie whispered.

"So? I'm sure it's no surprise to…*what* is wrong with Teddy?"

All three sisters turned, to the men standing on ladders at the other end of the historic church, hanging garlands already made. "What are you talking about?" Rebecca asked.

Susie frowned. "He keeps scratching his shoulder and arms and the back of his neck."

"I don't know," Amy replied. "Maybe he got poked by the branches when he was carrying them in," she theorized finally. "Although I've never known him to be allergic to plants."

"Forget that." Impatiently, Rebecca drew them back to the conversation at hand, instead of what was happening on the other side of the church. "You never answered the question, Amy," she pointed out. "What are you getting Teddy for Christmas?"

Amy shrugged and turned her attention to the group of women adding red velvet bows to the end of each pew, and the other setting up beautiful antique silver candelabra stands on either side of the altar. The chapel was going to be absolutely beautiful when it was finished being decorated. As beautiful as the music still wafting through the historic chapel. "I haven't really thought about it."

"You better start," Susie warned. "Christmas is only a week away."

"If anyone's asking, I recommend lingerie," Rebecca said.

Susie blew out an exasperated breath. "Talk about a one-track mind."

Rebecca shrugged. "Well, they *are* trying to have a baby."

Amy knew her very happily married older sisters were trying to help, but there were times when they needed to mind their own business. This was one of them. "I am not having this discussion!" Amy said stonily, and turned away. Then, to her great relief, she saw Teddy heading toward her.

Unfortunately, he looked anything but happy.

When he neared her, she saw why.

She gasped in horror. "What happened?" He had hives breaking out all over his neck and hands.

"Sorry to have to cut and run," Teddy said with a grimace, "but I've got to go to the emergency room. Now."

"IT'S AN ALLERGIC REACTION, all right," Amy's brother, Jeremy—the physician on call—confirmed in the Laramie Community Hospital emergency room. "Any idea what the culprit might be?"

Teddy winced and continued rubbing at his leg and chest. He moved his gaze away from Amy. "I'm guessing laundry detergent."

Amy flushed with a mixture of embarrassment and guilt. The nurse had made Teddy undress down to his birthday suit.

In an effort to minimize his embarrassment, Amy had turned her back while her husband put on the gown.

There was still a lot of skin exposed to her view. It was

obvious from the angry red welts covering his muscular arms and legs that the rash covered every inch clothing had touched. And since she had washed everything down to his underwear and socks…

With every second that passed, Teddy looked more itchy and uncomfortable.

"I've been allergic to everything but this one brand since I was a kid," Teddy continued.

A fact which made Amy feel all the worse. "You should have told me that!"

Teddy shrugged, the muscles in his brawny shoulders bunching against the thin fabric of the hospital gown. "You never asked." Frowning, he held up a hand before she could comment. "I'm sorry, Amy. That was uncalled-for," he said sincerely. "I get grumpy when I have an allergic outbreak like this."

Amy couldn't blame him. If Teddy felt even half as miserable as he looked…

Jeremy wrote on the chart. "The shot of antihistamine I'm ordering for you will help. Unfortunately, it's going to make you very sleepy."

Teddy mumbled something Amy was just as glad not to hear.

"The good news is that by morning," Jeremy continued, with his best bedside manner, "the hives should be completely gone."

"Thanks." Teddy nodded at her brother gratefully.

Jeremy looked at Amy and, unable to resist, teased, "Do me a favor, sis. Don't ever do *my* laundry."

"Hah, hah."

"Seriously," Jeremy continued with a provoking grin, before heading out the door. "With help like this…"

Amy shot him a withering glance.

Once Jeremy exited, Amy turned back to Teddy. "I really am sorry," she whispered.

He nodded, accepting her apology.

His kindness in the wake of such physical agony only made her feel all the worse.

The nurse came back in, syringe in hand, cutting off whatever else Amy could have said to make amends. Not that any statement she might make, however heartfelt, would do anything to erase her husband's discomfort.

So Amy took care of the insurance paperwork and made the co-pay. By the time she had finished, Teddy was dressed again and ready to go. To her relief the shot must have worked because he had already stopped itching as if he'd walked into a nest of mosquitoes.

"We have just enough time to get to the supermarket before they close for the night."

He shook off the suggestion. "It can wait."

Amy scoffed and took the keys from him. "Not unless you want to go buck naked or wear dirty clothing you brought home from your trip, it can't." She grinned, looped her arm through his and tilted her face up toward him. "I washed *everything,* remember?"

He chuckled and tugged her closer. "No one ever said you weren't thorough."

"SERIOUSLY, I'M FINE," TEDDY said when Amy parked next to the ranch house.

Sure he was, if his definition of fine was nodding off four times in the past forty minutes.

Amy vaulted out of the driver's seat and rushed around to help him with his door.

"I'm not an invalid," Teddy grumbled, continuing to resist her help.

And although Amy could hardly blame him for that—it was her "help" that had left him looking and feeling like a science experiment gone wrong—she also knew the only way she was going to make amends was by doing everything she could to alleviate his misery. Unfortunately, unless he started cooperating with her, she wasn't going to be able to do that.

She grabbed the extra-large bottle of hypoallergenic laundry detergent from behind the seat. "Jeremy and the nurse both said you should sleep this off."

He pried the heavy plastic bottle from her hand and wrapped his other arm around her shoulders. "Jeremy and the nurse weren't away from you for the past four days." He pulled her close to his side and nuzzled the top of her head. "I missed you. I want to spend time with you."

A thrill shifted through her, mingling with the sharper, more intense feelings of guilt. Honestly, what was she thinking? She could not take advantage of an ailing man. Not in good conscience, anyway. "Seriously, Teddy, get into bed."

His eyes lit up with the possibilities that could occur.

She thought about the way he'd been dozing off and on, while she dashed into the supermarket and drove back to the ranch. The one thing their marriage did not need was another attempt at lovemaking that did not quite pan out, for reasons relating to him this time. "Please," she implored, as if she found the whole idea ridiculous, which in reality she did not. "You're half-dead on your feet!"

He leered at her suggestively. "I could rally."

"I'm sure you could." Amy pushed away the memory of his slow, insistent kisses and tender caresses. He hadn't so much as kissed her and she could almost feel his hot, gentle hands on her body and the deep possessive way he thrust inside her. Arms and legs tensing with the need to hold him tight against her, she drew in a deep breath and tried to think rationally. She wrapped her arm about his waist and leaned her head against his shoulder. "But—"

He winced and lamented playfully, "Uh-oh. Here it comes."

"I want you well before I take advantage of you."

He gave her the thoughtful once-over and the heavy-lidded look that always presaged their lovemaking. She felt herself go weak in the knees.

"You're planning to take advantage of me?" he asked huskily.

If he only knew, Amy thought, as another ribbon of desire unfurled inside her. The nights he had been away, she had lain awake in that big bed, thinking about how nice it would be not just to make love with him—for pure fun this time—but to sleep next to him again, to feel his big strong body curled around hers and hear his deep, even breathing and drink in his musky male scent.

Making love only during the three days or so a month she was ovulating was simply not going to be enough to satisfy her. Or him, either, judging from the way he was looking at her.

"You'll have to wait and see." She paused as he took the key from her, set the detergent down and fumbled with the lock on the front door.

Another sign, she thought regretfully, of just how "drunk" with antihistamine he was.

"I don't know what you're going to sleep in, though…." She leaned against the entryway, contemplating his ruggedly handsome face and teasing smile.

He lifted a broad shoulder in an affable shrug. "Sheets would be nice," he ventured finally.

She returned his innocent look with a droll look of her own. "I meant clothing."

His lips curled upward in a sexy grin. "Who needs clothing?"

The thought of seeing him again, sans covering of any kind, in the privacy and sanctity of their bedroom, set her heart to racing.

"No pj's tonight," she said dryly, pointing him toward the bedroom, telling herself that no matter how much he tried to seduce her, they were not making love again until he was fully recovered.

For one thing, who knew what the friction of her naked body against his would do to those welts? She couldn't bear it if she started his itching again or inadvertently made the welts swell even more.

He hit the light switch on the wall as they walked in. "You're coming to keep me company?"

No doubt what he wanted to happen if she complied.

"Yes," Amy said, thinking there were other ways to make him comfortable. A cool drink. A snack. Maybe something interesting to read. "Just as soon as I get a load of clothes—with the proper detergent this time—in the washing machine."

He kissed the top of her head. "I'll be waiting."

Amy was sure he would be.

It took ten minutes to sort enough clothes to guarantee Teddy something to wear the next day, start the washer and prepare a tray in the kitchen. Only one to figure out he was already sound asleep by the time she entered the bedroom.

Chapter Ten

Amy woke to the feel of a hand on her shoulder, and Teddy standing over her. A sheet wrapped around his waist, he looked every bit as disheveled as she felt.

"What are you doing out here?" he murmured.

Slipping one arm beneath her shoulders, the other beneath her knees, he lifted her against his chest and carried her toward the bedroom. "I never meant for you to spend the night doing all my laundry again," he told her, laying her gently down onto the bed still warm from his body.

Amy hadn't meant to stay up most of the night, either.

But, given the desire flowing through her, and the worse-for-wear state of her husband, it had seemed wiser to sleep on the sofa.

"What time is it?" Amy asked drowsily, trying in vain to focus on the digital clock beside the bed.

"Early enough for you to catch forty more winks." Teddy covered her with the blankets.

Aware she wasn't going to be very productive unless she did get some rest, Amy gave into the overwhelming fatigue and drifted back to sleep.

When she woke again, sunlight was streaming through the blinds.

Teddy was coming toward her with a cup of steaming coffee in hand. "Ed called." He sat beside her on the bed. "Something about a prospective client coming by to visit Laurel Valley Ranch this afternoon?"

Stunned she could have forgotten that, Amy shoved the hair from her face and sat up. She breathed in the heady aroma of the coffee and took an enervating sip. "The owner of a chain of hardware stores in west Texas is looking for someone to supply him with starter plants for the spring planting. It would be a pretty big order."

Teddy set the mug on the bedside table. "He won't be there until one o'clock. Which gives you three hours. Otherwise, I probably would have just let you sleep."

Amy swung her feet over the side of the bed, started to stand and just as quickly felt the room tilt.

"Whoa." Teddy caught her with an arm around her waist.

He felt warm and strong and solid against her.

"You okay?"

Amy clung to his biceps. It took a moment to steady herself, but eventually the world righted. She laughed shakily. "I think I just got up too fast."

He studied her, his hazel eyes intent. "Sure?"

Amy drew a breath. "Yes." She drew another breath, wondering what was happening to her. She felt so... strange.

Tentatively, she let go of him, and found she could stand on her own after all. Deliberately, she shook off the wooziness. Maybe it was too much sleep, at the wrong time of day. Maybe her body clock was off. "I'm just going to go hop in the shower." She adapted her usual I-can-do-anything attitude.

Teddy smiled, looking relieved to see her heading

slowly—albeit purposefully—toward the master bath. "By the time you get out, I'll have breakfast ready."

He was as good as his word.

When she emerged from the bathroom, he was setting the table. The aroma of crisp fried bacon and fluffy golden pancakes filled the air. The griddle sizzled as he poured more pancake batter onto it.

"Go ahead and get started," he said, pulling the platter out of the warming oven. "I'll join you in a minute."

Amy sat down. By the time she had finished adding butter and maple syrup to her plate, Teddy had joined her.

In the laundry room beyond, Amy could see Teddy had continued rewashing his clothing. Judging from the piles on the floor, there was still a lot to go. She shook her head.

"I'm so sorry about what happened with the detergent."

His lips formed a half smile that was more amused than rueful. "Don't be. Besides, it's kind of funny."

Maybe now that his hives all appeared to be gone, and he'd stopped itching. She tried without much success to squelch her humiliation. The one time she tried to do something wifely, she had failed—big-time—and in front of both their families and many of their friends, no less. "I'm sure one day I'll think so," she replied.

He went easy on the butter, heavy on the syrup. "It's the thought that counts. And the impulse was really sweet. Although—" he paused to look her in the eye "—just for the record, I don't expect you to do my laundry just because you're my wife."

Amy gulped, feeling like a failure again. "I know." Teddy was as independent as she was.

He studied her while he chewed. "But…?"

She ducked her head. "I thought it would be nice if we felt like more of a team," she said shyly.

He shifted in his chair and leaned toward her, his knees nudging hers under the table. He captured her hand in his, squeezed with a familiarity that somehow felt more intimate than friendly. "Then, in that case, I owe you a lot of laundry." A warm, welcoming smile spread across his handsome face. "Because I want all chores to be shared around here."

Amy returned the playful look and wrinkled her nose at him. "I'm not sure I could wait until everything in my closet was in need of laundering, cowboy."

He chuckled but made no promise to change his way of handling his dirty clothing. "Then I'll have to think of some other way to pull my weight around here, make it a more 'equal effort' household."

ALWAYS A MAN OF HIS WORD, Teddy got started that very afternoon. Or at least he tried to step up to the responsibilities of marriage—of becoming a team—a little more. It was hard to do when his wife was not cooperating.

Nevertheless, he kept trying, kept leaving messages for her.

"Amy? It's Teddy. I was thinking we could have dinner in town this evening, so call me back."

"Hey, Amy. Your husband again. Haven't heard from you. I know you're busy with a client this afternoon, but when you're done, call me back so we can settle on our plans for this evening. I'd really like to take you out."

"Amy." Teddy tried but couldn't keep the tension from his voice. "I'm beginning to get a little worried. Call me back."

But she didn't return his calls, and the ranch house was dark when Teddy walked in at six o'clock that evening.

Amy still wasn't answering her cell phone or returning her messages. Nor was she answering the phone in her trailer at her ranch.

It was possible, of course, that she wasn't carrying her cell or near enough to her other phone to hear it ring, and hence, hadn't gotten any of his messages.

It was also possible something had happened.

Teddy grabbed his keys and headed right back out.

To his relief, although the trailer was dark, the lights were on in one of Amy's greenhouses at her ranch. He parked beside it and walked in to find her pouring potting soil into flats of black vinyl snap-apart starter pots. She had her earphones on and was obviously listening to her MP3 player as she worked, which explained why she hadn't heard him drive up or come in. Probably why she wasn't answering her phone, either. His fear and exasperation faded, replaced by relief.

"Amy!" he shouted.

She didn't respond.

He strode closer, tapped her on her shoulder. "Amy!"

Startled, she jumped.

When she saw who it was, she glared at him and took one of the earphones out of her ear. "You scared me half to death!" she grumbled.

He refused to apologize for behaving like a husband whose wife may have been in some sort of trouble. "I was worried about you," he told her gruffly.

"Oh. Sorry." Briefly, guilt shimmered in her pretty eyes. "I guess I should have called you to tell you I'd be late getting home tonight."

And listened to your messages, Teddy thought.

"But once I got started on this, I guess I lost track of everything else."

No kidding. "I want to take you out for dinner tonight," he said patiently.

"I wish I could." Her eyes filled with regret. "But I

can't. I got an order for six thousand starter plants, due in February. Which means I've got to get the seedlings going in the next two weeks, and with Christmas and New Year's coming up, and Ed and Sheryl expecting their baby at some point in the next couple of weeks, too…"

"Where is Ed?" Teddy interrupted. Maybe it was Neanderthal of him, but he didn't like the idea of Amy shouldering this all alone.

"He had to take Sheryl to a doctor's appointment at three-thirty this afternoon. It was just routine—she's been doing a lot better since she's been on bed rest—but I told him not to come back."

Teddy respected Amy for putting the personal needs of her employees above the demands of her business. It was the hallmark of a good boss. However, shortsightedness was not. "So why didn't you call me?" he asked, leaning against the potting table and folding his arms in front of him.

She blinked, as if confused.

"I would have lent a hand," he continued.

Amy scoffed and went back to pouring potting soil into trays. "You have your horses."

Teddy shrugged. "So I'll take care of my own business and then come over to help you."

Her lower lip slid out. She was even prettier, he noted, when she was stubborn. "You don't have to do this."

Yeah, he did. For so many reasons. Most of which had to do with his soul-deep need to shelter and protect her. "We're not just friends now, Amy," he reminded her softly. "We're married. That makes us a team in every way. Whatever you need, tell me, I'll help you. And I promise to do the same with you."

"Even when it comes to our businesses?"

"Even then."

She held his eyes, weighed it over. Finally she smiled and handed him a pair of leather work gloves and a waterproof apron. "In that case, in order to keep to the schedule I've set for myself, we need to get another three hundred seeds planted before I call it quits for the night."

TO AMY'S DELIGHT, TEDDY was as adept with soil as he was with horses. With him measuring planting mix into the starter trays, and her carefully adding seeds and moisture, they were finished by eight-thirty that evening.

"I don't know about you, but I'm famished." Amy yanked off her gloves and apron and led the way out of the greenhouse.

"Me, too." He adjusted his longer strides to hers and smiled down at her. "Still want to go into town for dinner?"

"I don't think I can wait that long." Amy averted her eyes from the tempting proximity of his sensually chiseled lips. Aware they were getting very used to being together this way, behaving like a couple, she asked, "Would you mind if we rustled up something here?"

"No problem."

Aware how good it felt to have Teddy so close at hand, Amy strolled into the trailer. She flipped on the lights, paused just long enough to wash her hands, and then went straight to the fridge. She studied the contents with disappointment. "Pickin's are slim, I'm afraid." Hoping for better luck, she opened up the cupboard that served as her pantry.

Teddy came up behind her, still drying his hands on a dish towel.

The steamy atmosphere of her greenhouse had kinked up the ends of his reddish-brown hair. Evening beard clung to his jaw. The combination was heartthrob—cute and sexy.

He looked past her and beamed. "Are you kidding me? We can have a feast."

"One of us needs glasses."

Teddy plucked out a can of cream of chicken soup and another of stewed tomatoes with green chilies from the cupboard, grated Mexican-blend cheese and a package of pre-grilled southwestern chicken strips she used on her lunchtime salads from the fridge. "Adjust the oven so it heats to 350," he said.

Amy made a quick calculation. "I see where you're going with this," she said with a grin.

He grabbed two vegetables from the wire basket on the counter. "Then you won't mind heating up a fry pan with a little olive oil, while I dice green pepper and onion."

Short minutes later, the trailer was filled with the aroma of sizzling vegetables. Working like a well-oiled team, they assembled their version of King Ranch casserole, and slid it into the oven to bake.

Teddy poured bagged salad onto plates. Amy got out the ranch-style salad dressing and a jar of green olives.

Teddy made a face as she downed three olives in quick succession. She chuckled as she settled opposite him in the booth that served as her dining area in the small space. "I forgot how much you loathed olives."

He nodded. "Ripe or green."

Amy downed several more. "They're good," she insisted.

"I'll take your word for it," he replied.

Amy leaned back in her seat, aware now that she'd munched on something savory, she really wanted something sweet.

Figuring "dessert" should wait until after their entrée, she sighed and dug into her salad. "Don't forget. We've got Sheryl and Ed's couples baby shower coming up."

"When is it?"

"Saturday afternoon." Amy's craving for chocolate remained unabated. "At 2:00 p.m."

Amy got up and rummaged in the cupboard until she found a bag of semisweet baking morsels.

She opened the package and quaffed a few, then offered it to Teddy. He shook his head wordlessly and kept on eating his salad—but not before giving her a weird look.

"Did we get a gift?" he asked.

Amy sat back down again and began eating her greens.

Now she wanted olives again.

Which wasn't surprising.

When she let herself get too hungry, she tended to crave—and eat—a little bit of everything. Especially when she was waiting for her dinner to finish cooking.

Aware Teddy was waiting for an answer, she said, "Yes, we got them a gift. We are giving them the bouncy chair they registered for."

Finished with his salad, he pushed his plate away and relaxed against the back of the eating booth. As he shifted, their knees touched. He did not pull away and Amy tingled warmly where their bodies meshed.

"Thanks for taking care of that for me—us."

Amy smiled. "You're welcome." Their eyes met, held. A different kind of heat started deep inside her, one that seemed to arrow straight for the bedroom and her cozy double bed.

Aware recreational sex was part of their deal with each other now, although they had yet to really take advantage of the impulsive shift in house rules, she looked down at her plate and said, "Thanks for helping me tonight."

He reached over to cover her hand with his. "You're welcome," he said softly.

Silence fell as Amy's heartbeat kicked up another notch—followed swiftly by her libido.

"I'll write you a check for my half," Teddy continued seriously.

Amy was about to say, "You don't have to do that," when she realized as per their informal prenuptial agreement to keep their finances separate, they sort of did.

Teddy released his physical hold on her but kept right on looking at her, as intently as if he were memorizing every facet of her face.

"Amazing," he informed her casually, with a shake of his head, "how much I missed you when I was away this week."

Me, too.

Amy had never expected to be so lonely.

"What's amazing," she said with as much flippancy as she could muster, "is how well we're beginning to adjust to this whole marriage business."

He inclined his head to one side. "Agreed."

"At first…" Amy paused, bit her lip.

"I know." He held up a hand. "I wasn't sure it was going to work, either."

And yet…now… "I'm beginning to think it will."

He nodded with contentment. "Me, too."

Would wonders never cease?

"You can't possibly want anything more to eat," Teddy chided, half an hour later.

"Actually—" Amy went back to the cupboard again, rummaging through what was there "—I kind of do."

Not really seeing anything that appealed to her, she

went to the fridge and then the freezer. "Aha!" She pulled out a small carton of rocky road from behind half a sack of frozen peas. "This is what I need."

Teddy lifted a skeptical brow. He carried the empty casserole and plates to the sink and turned on the faucet.

Amy lounged against the counter while she pried off the frosty top. She dug her spoon into the marshmallow popping out of the top of the chocolate-and-nut-studded ice cream. She waved the first luscious bite in his direction. "Want some?"

"No." Amusement gleamed in his eyes. "Thanks. I'm stuffed."

Amy let the rich dessert melt on her tongue and found it did indeed hit the spot. "Wimp," she teased.

Teddy did the dishes with the same quick efficiency he did everything else that had to be done domestically. "And they talk about men having cast-iron stomachs." He rolled his eyes.

"It's strange." Amy dug out another big bite. "Sometimes I'm really hungry." She savored the confection. When it had melted away, she crunched on a nut. "Other times I'm not."

"As opposed to me, who's always a certain level of hungry." Teddy let the sudsy water out of the sink and hung up the dish towel.

Amy took another, smaller bite. "Must be the male hormone," she theorized.

Teddy shrugged, speculating, "Or the caloric demands of the male body."

Beginning to feel a little stuffed, Amy put the carton back in the freezer. She had the absurd urge to curl up in a ball and go to sleep. And another, strong desire to…

"Satisfied now?" Teddy asked, interrupting her reverie.

Amy nodded, contemplating the forbidden nature of her thoughts. "Almost, yeah."

Another lift of that handsome brow.

Amy's heart skipped a beat at the blatant sexuality in his gaze. She hitched in a deep, galvanizing breath.

"What I'd really like now is a hot, steamy shower." Her low voice vibrated in the soft silence of the evening.

She grabbed the front of his shirt and tugged him close. Deciding there was no time like the present to satisfy her every need, she said, "And one more thing."

"That being?" he queried huskily, looking deep into her eyes.

Amy smiled. "This."

AMY COULDN'T BELIEVE WHAT had gotten into her as she initiated the kiss. She had never been a particularly sexual person. Never imagined feeling this way about any man, never mind the guy who had been her best male friend.

Living with him, working with him, playing with him and, yes, even trying to make a baby with him had changed all that. She could not look at Teddy now, stand next to him or eat a meal with him and not notice everything about him. Like how good he smelled. Or how fit and strong he was. How gentle, tender and caring.

Her pulse fluttering in anticipation, she rose on tiptoe. He met her halfway and her lips were inundated with a kiss that started out hard and deep, and then switched gears to sweet and slow.

Aware how small the bathroom was, she began unbuttoning his shirt in the hall. When she had it off, his T-shirt, jeans and boots came next. He leaned against the wall, watching as she stripped him of everything including his briefs.

"My turn." He caught her hands when she'd finished, drawing her to her feet.

She shuddered as he removed her outer clothes, then fell to his knees in front of her. He pressed a kiss just above the top of her thong.

"The shower," she whispered.

"We'll get there." He stroked the sensitive insides of her thighs, from knees to pelvis, and back again. Sliding his fingers beneath the elastic, he traced the petal softness with his fingertips, and the dampness that flowed. "Right now I want to love you."

Amy quivered, already sliding toward the edge. His lips followed, tracing a path of fire. Not sure she could take much more, Amy whispered, "Oh, Teddy…"

He chuckled in triumph and brought her closer yet, sliding her thong all the way down and off. Using the pads of his fingertips, he traced every feminine curve, every sweet, sensitive spot, until she was swaying against him mindlessly, aware no one had ever desired her in such a fundamental way. She'd thought they could separate baby-making from lovemaking, casual sex from married sex, but as he stood again and took her all the way into his arms and began kissing her once again, she knew it was all one and the same. She couldn't make love to him like this without loving him. She couldn't be with him like this and not surrender to the feelings, the possibilities, the future. Their future…

Teddy had known if they made love the way he wanted to, with no restrictions, that it would deepen their relationship. But even as he removed her bra and caressed her breasts, even as he brought her closer yet, so they were pressed intimately together and his lips found hers again, he knew it was a whole lot more.

He wanted Amy in his life, not just as a wife to give him the baby they both wanted, but as a mate he could go through life with. He wanted her in his arms, kissing him, just like this. He wanted her so eager to make love with him that she couldn't wait to get their clothes off.

He let his hand slide through the hair at the nape of her neck, and the way she responded with such sweet vulnerability made his heart pound. She groaned as his tongue found its way into her mouth and tangled with his.

Still kissing her, he danced her backward toward the shower. She had a dazed look in her eyes as he reached behind her and turned on the water. It splattered over them, so cold at first it made them laugh and catch their breath. And then his lips were on hers again. He brought her flush against him, pouring everything he had into the kiss, everything he felt, everything he wanted and needed. She kissed him back with everything she possessed. His body heated, as surely as the water sluicing over them, and still he kept stroking her. He wanted Amy to feel the power of their attraction to each other as intently as he did. To his delight, her nipples budded against his chest. Lower still, he cupped her with his hand and she arched against him, even as her knees faltered. Her passionate response sent need throbbing to his groin.

"Now, Teddy," she whispered, wrapping her legs around his waist. "Now…"

The vee of her thighs cradled his hardness, welcoming him inside. She moved against him once again. He heard her moan and felt her closing tight and then it was just too much. There was only this incredible gift, the connection of heart, soul and mind. He plunged deep, protecting and possessing her even as she seduced and surrendered. Their joining was as tender and loving as it was full of fire and passion. Christmas, Teddy thought, really had come early this year.

Chapter Eleven

"You lucked out," Amy informed Teddy Saturday afternoon as they hit the Laramie city limits and found their way through peaceful, tree-lined streets to Ed and Sheryl's bungalow. "You don't have to participate in any of the games."

Teddy shot Amy a surprised glance from behind the wheel.

Party games had never been of any interest to him. Probably because he had no patience for useless trivia. Psychologically revealing contests were even worse, in his estimation.

Once again, she'd read his mind. "How did you know I was dreading that?" he teased.

Amy wrinkled her nose. Her eyes danced merrily. "I've yet to meet a man who's enthused about participating in these types of games, but they're a requirement for all the women, so…"

Her suede jacket hung open, revealing her subtle curves and slender body. Lazily, he let his gaze slide over her red turtleneck sweater, form-fitting jeans and heeled Western boots. "Maybe if they were athletic contests," he offered. "Or poker…"

Amy scoffed. "Not going to happen at a baby shower,

cowboy. Anyway, because each couple forms a team and I am running the games, you wouldn't have a partner, so instead *you*—" she reached over and tapped his chest, then hers "—get to assist *me*."

"Nothing I'd rather do than that." He reached over and squeezed her knee.

Amy cocked her head to one side. Her honey-blond curls slipped across her cheek. "Hear that?" she said.

Teddy listened.

A few blocks over, melodic peals filled the air, announcing the hour.

Teddy smiled at the familiar sound that had been absent the past month. "They must have finished installing the bell in the clock tower on the community chapel this morning." All the churches in the area had bells of some sort. Only the one in historic downtown Laramie announced the time four times every hour.

Amy's face lit up. "Just in time for the twins' christening tomorrow afternoon, and the Christmas services."

Teddy took Amy's hand as they headed up the sidewalk toward the front door after parking the car. The future was looking up.

To Teddy's relief, the couples' baby shower was a lot less stilted and girlie than he had imagined. The very pregnant Sheryl was still on bed rest, so she was confined to a hospital bed set up in the living room, while her husband Ed and mother, Dorothy, kept a watchful eye on her and made sure she had everything she needed.

Amy was in her element, running games like Identify That Nursery Item, Name That Lullaby, and Favorite Children's Stories Crosswords. All Teddy had to do was pass out papers and pens, help tabulate scores and give out prizes.

A cinch, he thought, until he started to collect the pads and pens.

"Hold on there. We're not done yet," Dorothy interjected.

Sheryl smiled. "Mom and I don't want Teddy and Amy to miss out on all the fun. We want them to be able to participate in a game, too, so we've got a *Newlywed* magazine quiz for everyone to take. And pay attention and give it your best shot, everybody, because the grand prize is a dinner for two!"

Ed grinned—probably because he didn't have to participate in this, Teddy thought—and passed out copies of the game to all the contestants, along with paper and pen for Amy and Teddy.

"I've never come out ahead in one of these quizzes I've taken yet," Teddy's brother, Trevor, muttered as he stared down at the list of fill-in-the-blank questions.

"No one has," another guy quipped.

"Now hush and just get down to business," Dorothy scolded in a lively maternal tone. "You've only got ten minutes. And remember, everyone, it's important you don't see what your spouse is writing, because we'll be comparing your answers to come up with the final scores."

Even better, Teddy thought, thinking it couldn't get any worse.

Again, he was wrong.

Minutes later, the buzzer went off, signaling time was up.

He had the feeling he was about to be humiliated—badly.

"Now, we're going to read everyone's answers out loud," Dorothy smiled. "Teddy. You and Amy are first."

The wife's favorite breakfast cereal and husband's favorite sport weren't so bad. Nor were the questions about most-watched television shows, hobbies, pets and colors. It was the last two Teddy could have done without.

"When was y'all's first kiss. Amy?"

Amy blushed. "We were stuck in an ice storm."

"Teddy? Your answer?"

Teddy looked down at the paper in his hand and read his answer. "Uh—our wedding day."

Blinks, all around.

Clearly, no one had expected that.

Worse than the fact that Amy and Teddy hadn't agreed on when their first kiss had occurred, how was it possible, they were all clearly wondering, that Amy and Teddy hadn't even kissed each other until after they'd said their vows? Who wouldn't want to at least test-drive a kiss or two…or three before committing to someone else for the rest of their lives…?

"Okay." Dorothy composed herself and offered a gracious smile. "Let's go on to the final question. When did you know he or she was The One for you? Teddy? Do you want to give us your answer?"

"Easy," he said, gazing into her eyes, wordlessly beseeching her not to care what anyone else thought about their actions. "It was the day I asked Amy to marry me," he said softly, thinking that was when everything good in his life had really begun.

Unfortunately, the startled, unhappy look in Amy's eyes indicated he had given the wrong answer, once again.

"Amy?" Dorothy asked, her expression curious. "Do you want to tell us when it was you knew Teddy was The One for you?"

Amy blushed all the harder. Although she was trying hard to hide it, Teddy could see that she was as miserable as he. "I said it was the first time we, um… hooked up."

AMY'S FACE STILL FELT AS IF it was on fire, fifteen minutes later, when the prize for the Newlywed Quiz had been given out. To her relief, she and Teddy were finally able to escape to the kitchen to make coffee and prepare the cake for serving.

"Sorry about that," Teddy apologized the minute they were alone.

In the living room, there were oohs and aahs as baby gifts were opened.

Trying hard not to think what Teddy's last two answers really meant, never mind what her own revealed, Amy concentrated on spooning coffee into the filter.

"Sorry for what?" She measured water with equal precision.

Teddy clamped his hands on her shoulders and turned her to face him. "I'm sorry for only managing to get fifty percent of my answers to match yours," he repeated.

Aware her skin was tingling beneath the warm pressure of his hands, Amy shrugged and pretended an inner ease she couldn't begin to feel. "You didn't know what I was thinking." For both their sakes, she gave him an easy out. It wasn't his fault he clearly had never decided she was The One, at least not in the way the Newlywed Quiz question had meant.

Teddy frowned, apparently thinking she was just upset because they had lost out on the dinner-for-two grand prize. "Still." He counted out coffee cups for all the guests. "I should have realized our first kiss was a real kiss—not the one we laid on each other at the wedding."

"It's okay. Really." She held up a hand to stave off further physical contact and went to the refrigerator.

Holding the door open with her hip, she lifted out the sheet cake, set it on the island and opened the bakery-box lid. As the scent of lemon and butter-cream frosting assaulted her, she felt a sudden, unexpected wave of nausea. Which was weird. She loved butter cream and lemon.

Fortunately, Teddy was right there, to help her ease the sheet cake onto the crystal serving platter on the counter.

Holding her breath so as not to inhale the rich aromas again, Amy backed away. She busied herself getting out the plates and silverware to go along with the coffee cups.

"And the last question," Teddy continued, heaping napkins onto a serving tray. "The one about when he knew we were meant to be together. That was even more of a loss, as far as I was concerned." He thrust a hand through his hair. "How are we supposed to just come up with stuff like that on the spur of the moment?"

It wouldn't have been a problem, Amy thought disparagingly, had they been a normal couple.

She turned away from his probing gaze once again. "It was just for fun, Teddy." She shrugged and concentrated on the task of serving refreshments. "So our answers didn't match nearly as much as anyone else's. We shouldn't let it upset us."

What did upset Amy was the knowledge that her feelings for Teddy had changed during the weeks they had been married. Clearly, Teddy's feelings for her, hadn't. It didn't mean they couldn't. They just hadn't so far.

"And yet," he said, clearly forgetting for a moment what they were supposed to be doing and taking her in his arms. "It is bothering you."

Well, heck, yes, it was. Her feelings were hurt. She felt like she had when she'd been in middle school and she was the only one in her social group who didn't have a boyfriend. It still stung to recall the memory of standing along the gymnasium wall all night, while everyone else happily paired off on the dance floor.

Now, practically everyone else she was close to had found their soul mates, and here she was, feeling unrequited love for the man she was married to.

It shouldn't hurt so much.

But it did.

But how could she tell Teddy that, without ruining what they had?

He had more than held up his end of the bargain thus far.

In fact, so far he had been a damn good husband.

She was the one trying to change the rules on them, midmarriage.

The one wanting the impossible.

Aware he was studying her with a peculiar look on his face now—the kind that said he wondered if she was flipping out or something—Amy swallowed hard and pushed all her inner angst aside.

"So I don't like coming in dead last, in anything," Amy fibbed, feigning the kind of hypercompetitiveness she hadn't felt since she was a kid. She forced merriment into her eyes. "We'll learn all that stuff about each other eventually. And have fun doing it."

He continued regarding her skeptically.

As if he didn't quite believe her but wasn't going to call her on it, either.

Not here. Not now.

"Now you're talking," Teddy said.

Pulse racing, she turned away. He caught her gently but determinedly by the shoulder and brought her back around to face him.

He lowered his head to hers. Their lips met in an explosion of heat and need, softness and pleasure.

Who knew how long they would have stood there, locked in each other's arms, Amy thought wistfully, had it not been for the swift sound of approaching footsteps and an eruption of deep male laughter.

"I'll tell you what's taking so long with the refreshments," Tyler McCabe's familiar voice called, to one and all. "They're in here! Making out again!"

More laughter emerged from the other room. Teddy and Amy broke apart again. She flushed in embarrassment as Tyler shook his head at Teddy and discreetly disappeared back into the living room.

"See?" Teddy grinned, all triumphant testosterone-laced male. He brought her to him for an extra-affectionate hug. "We're ahead of the pack on something, already."

"I DON'T KNOW ABOUT LEAVING you," Dorothy told her daughter.

Sheryl put a hand beneath her back and tried to get more comfortable in the bed for what seemed the umpteenth time in fifteen minutes. "I'll feel worse if you pass up this chance to get out with Ed and do a little Christmas shopping."

"But what if…?"

Sheryl accepted the extra pillow her husband brought her and slid it behind her lower back. That done, she adjusted the hospital bed to a slightly higher slant. "Teddy and Amy are going to be here with me. Please. Just go." She looked at them pleadingly. "And have a good time."

"Okay," Ed finally relented, "but I've got my cell if you need me."

"I'm not going into labor today. I promise. Now go." Sheryl made shooing motions toward the door.

Reluctantly, her husband and her mother said goodbye and left.

"What kind of pizza do you ladies want for dinner?" Teddy asked.

Sheryl rubbed her stomach, as if she were ravenous. "I don't care as long as it has pepperoni. I've got to have pepperoni. And lots of cheese."

Teddy flashed a smile. "Caesar or garden salad?"

"Both."

"You got it." Teddy paused to draw Amy to him and kiss her cheek. "Back in a flash. And I've got my cell phone, too."

Sheryl let out a sigh as soon as she and Amy were alone. "I know people mean well…"

"But they're hovering," Amy sympathized.

Sheryl nodded. "I was just at the doctor's the other day, and she said it could be any time or it could be two weeks from today. They just don't know. The good news is the baby's lungs are developed so if I do deliver a week or two early, it shouldn't be a problem. Now, if I could just find a way to get comfortable and make this darn backache go away…"

"Can you use a heating pad or something?"

"It doesn't help. Nothing helps. I've just been lying prone for too long." Sheryl shifted again, so she was lying slightly on one side, then murmured in relief.

"Is that the only problem you've been having?" Amy asked, aware Sheryl still had that glow all pregnant women seemed to have.

"Unfortunately, no." Sheryl made a face. "I've also had nonstop heartburn. Swollen ankles. A bursting bladder, and, of course, the inability to get much real sleep no matter how hard I try."

"Has it been like that for your whole pregnancy or just since you went on bed rest?"

Sheryl thought for a moment. "I guess most of that has happened in the second and third trimester. The first trimester, in retrospect, was a lot easier for me once I got the morning sickness under control."

"What else bothered you in the beginning?" Amy asked as she continued stacking the shower gifts.

Amy knew she could go out and get a book on pregnancy, but that seemed like tempting fate. She wanted to have Teddy's baby so badly and she didn't want to jinx it.

"Oh, gosh." Sheryl shifted again, rubbing her lower back slowly. "I think the question those first few weeks was what didn't bother me. I was moody and sleepy and light-headed. I had these strange cravings, and I was nauseated by the weirdest things. Although the worst thing of all was the crying jags. Drop of a hat—" Sheryl snapped her fingers "—I'd be in tears." She paused and looked at Amy curiously. "Why do you ask?"

Amy shrugged and continued in a low, admiring voice, "You made it look so easy. I mean, one day you and Ed announced you were going to be starting a family as soon as possible. Two months later, a baby was on the way. I just wondered if you did anything special to, um, facilitate that."

Sheryl chuckled, reminiscing about the fun part of conceiving a child. "No. We just tried to relax and concentrate on how much we loved each other. We—aah!" Sheryl sat up abruptly, blinked. Put a hand to her belly. "Oh, no."

There was a dripping sound as moisture hit the floor.

"Don't look now," she said miserably, "but my water just broke!"

Amy went to get some towels. Then she gave Sheryl the phone. She dialed Ed's cell. "If you want to say you were right, you can," she said with a smile. "Yes. It's time. Turn back and we'll go to the hospital. Okay, bye, hon. Drive safe."

Sheryl ended the connection.

Just as suddenly, Amy noted the mother-to-be was looking awfully pale.

And then suddenly, almost berry-red.

Sheryl let out another moan. "I *really* think I need to get up."

Amy was at her side. Arm around her waist, she helped her to her feet.

"Oh…my…gosh…!" Sheryl gasped. "I think I feel the baby's head!"

It was impossible, Amy knew, for a baby to get into the birth canal that fast.

But because the by-now-moaning-and-shrieking Sheryl was insisting, Amy helped her back onto the bed, eased the clothing off her lower half and took a look.

"Oh, my heavens. You're right!" Amy said, beginning to feel a little frantic herself. "I've got to call 9-1-1!"

"No!" Sheryl grabbed Amy's wrist and wouldn't let go. "The baby's coming *right now!*" She shrieked again and began to push.

More water gushed out. And then the baby crowned.

The closest Amy had ever been to a live birth was the emergency childbirth video she'd had to watch in health class, years ago, but to her relief she remembered how to put her hand under the baby's head and gently support it as it worked its way out.

"Push again, Sheryl," Amy said.

Sheryl complied. And the next thing Amy knew, the baby's neck and shoulders were out. Another hard push and shriek from Sheryl and the torso and legs slid out.

Amy's heart pounded as she noted the baby wasn't moving. Or, it seemed, breathing.

Doing her best to keep her wits about her, Amy quickly cleared the baby's mouth of mucus with her fingertip.

As soon as it was clear, the baby let out a resounding cry.

Amy breathed a sigh of relief. She had never heard a more beautiful sound in all her life.

"I KNOW I'VE ASKED THIS three times already, but are you *sure* you're okay?" Teddy guided his pickup truck into the parking space and cut the engine.

Amy choked back a sob. "Of course."

"Then why are you still crying?" he asked her tenderly.

I'll be darned if I know. Amy stiffened her shoulders with as much dignity as she could muster. "I'm not really crying."

Teddy inclined his head to one side and peered at her closely. "Well, there's something coming out of your eyes."

Leave it to him to make a joke now of all times. Although it had lightened the tension…. Amy wiped the tissue across her cheeks. "It's just a reaction to all the adrenaline," she explained. "It'll pass in a minute." *I think.*

Teddy's expression morphed from concern to respect. He took her hand in his and kissed the inside of her wrist. "You did do an amazing job staying calm and delivering little Brian."

Amy closed her eyes and let her head rest against the back of the seat. "Hard to believe Sheryl didn't know she was having her baby. But that's the thing about silent back labor, the EMS techs said. You don't know you're in the process of giving birth until it's an indisputable fact."

Teddy released his lap belt and pulled her into the warm, welcoming curve of his body. "In any case," he said softly, gently stroking her hair with the flat of his hand, "all's well that ends well."

Amy nodded as a fresh flow of moisture escaped the corners of her eyes. Ed and Dorothy had arrived in time to go to the hospital with Sheryl and Brian. Teddy and Amy had stayed behind to clean up. Now it was time for them to go on their previously scheduled second "date night," as a married couple.

Although, as they sat in the parking lot of the theater where the movie was playing, Amy wasn't sure it was such a good idea. This year's Christmas movie blockbuster was supposed to be a real tearjerker. The last thing she needed was more fuel for her sudden onslaught of weepiness.

"I know it was your turn to plan our evening, and this is what you selected, but if you want to change the venue—" he watched her fish yet another tissue out of her purse and blow her nose "—I'm okay with that."

Amy nodded. She put a hand over her eyes as she felt another flood start.

"Sorry," she said thickly, wishing she would run out of tears before she drowned them both. "It's not like me to be this over-the-top emotional."

"I don't know much about this stuff. That's the problem with not having any sisters. But—could this be a hormonal surge?"

Was he thinking she might be pregnant, too? What was it Sheryl had said? *"Worst thing of all was the crying jags. Drop of a hat, I'd be in tears."*

Was that what this was? Amy wondered, by turns elated and confused.

She knew she'd been moody, sleepy and light-headed. She'd been craving things that were sour and sweet, and nearly heaved when she had caught a whiff of butter-cream frosting.

If she and Teddy *hadn't* conceived, her period was due about now. It was hard to say exactly when, since she had never had been all that regular with her cycle.

"I know you're not supposed to talk about PMS," he continued, as if worried he had overstepped, even bringing it up.

"You're right," Amy interrupted, not about to go down this road with him. It was too delicate a matter for them to tackle, especially when she was in this state of mind. "If a guy is smart, he won't mention it to the woman in his life."

"But if that's what is going on," Teddy persisted doggedly, "if that is what you think is about to happen, it's okay, Amy." Compassion softened his handsome features. "I went into this knowing it might take a while for us to have that baby we both want. And I'm perfectly willing to keep trying."

His words were sweet and comforting.

Plus, she loved making love with him, too. Maybe too much for her own good. What if she loved him too much and he never loved her back? she wondered anxiously. What if all he ever really wanted from her was friendship? Would she be able to live with that kind of emotional return from him?

Loving someone was supposed to be an end in itself. And it was. But, she was beginning to see, there was a part of her that needed to be loved back every bit as much as she needed to be able to give love to someone else.

Aware he was waiting for an answer, she said, "That's good to know." She swallowed around the tension in her throat and looked out the windshield.

He studied her in silence, looking every bit as off-kilter as she felt.

"That's not it, is it?" he deduced wryly, after a minute. "It's not PMS getting you down."

Amy wanted to tell him there was a chance the two of them had conceived the first time out of the gate. She was also afraid of jinxing it by speaking too soon. She certainly didn't want to get his hopes up, only to have to crush them a day or so later. Bad enough, she was feeling this way. Elated one minute, scared to death the next. Sad and uncertain after that.

The smart thing to do would be to get a test from the drugstore. Find out what the truth was. Then tell him whatever the case was.

"No," she said calmly, surprised to find her tears had finally vanished, as inexplicably and without warning as they had come, "it's not."

TEDDY KNEW AMY WAS withholding every bit as much as she was telling him. He also knew, from the stubbornly aloof glint in her brown eyes that he wasn't going to get any more out of her that evening.

Therefore, it was a relief when she said she wanted to go ahead with their original plans and see the movie, even though they had missed the previews and opening credits. It was a mystery how she managed to stay completely dry-eyed during a denouement that left him with a lump in his throat.

But then, maybe she had cried herself out after the ambulance had left and the enormity of what she had been through, delivering a baby with no help or advice whatsoever, hit her.

In any case, he knew that he needed to offer comfort in whatever way he could.

"Sleepy?" he asked, parking in the drive next to the ranch house.

She shrugged, looking every bit as reluctant to go into the house as he. "Not really."

"Me, neither." He rested one hand on top of the steering wheel, contemplating how best to get them both back in the Christmas spirit. "Want to go look at the stars and pretend we're in for some snow?"

"Sure." A wistful expression softened her eyes. "Why not."

Glad he'd done something right, Teddy said, "Be right back."

He left the motor running and disappeared into the ranch house. It took a few minutes to get everything together. He returned with an adjustable, battery-powered camping lantern, self-inflating air mattress, sleeping bag, blanket and a couple of pillows.

He tossed it all in the back of the truck, then climbed behind the wheel.

"Now I'm curious," Amy said with a smile.

Teddy winked. "Good."

Like him, she seemed to be struggling to define what their relationship had become. "Exactly what do you have in mind?"

"You'll see," he replied, moving a strand of hair from her face and tucking it behind her ear.

He felt her tremble at his touch and an answering response awakened inside him.

He was pretty sure she wanted him as much as he wanted her. And equally certain it would be a mistake to rush into intimacy again.

Reluctantly, he dropped his hand, shifted into gear and drove slowly through open pasture, until he reached what he felt was the prettiest place in the dead center of his ranch. It was away from the road, nestled by trees on all sides, yet open to the sky.

"You know what we haven't talked about?" Teddy asked, parking and getting out of the truck.

Amy followed, looking curious. Thrusting her hands in the pockets of her suede jacket, she watched as he unlatched the tailgate, turned on the camping lantern and set it down in the truck bed.

"Haven't a clue," she responded.

Teddy climbed up into the bed of the truck. Kneeling, he unrolled the air mattress and pushed the valve to make it self-inflate.

"We haven't talked about what you and I are going to get each other for Christmas." Teddy unzipped the sleeping bag and spread it over the air mattress. He tossed the pillows at the end next to the cab, then reached down to give her a hand up. "And with it only three days away now, it's about time we discussed it, don't you think?"

Teddy guided her into a prone position. He waited until she got comfortable, then turned the lantern down to night-light strength, stretched out beside her and pulled the soft wool blanket over them.

He propped his hands behind his head and looked up at the sky. It was an incredibly beautiful night, with a star-lit sky and a three-quarter moon.

"Usually we just give each other gift certificates to the hardware store," Amy said.

The mattress was very comfortable, but meant for one. As they shifted around, they quickly realized the only way they could get comfortable was by having Amy cuddle up next to him and rest her head on his shoulder.

Maybe it was hokey, Teddy thought, but he loved lying next to her this way. Loved just spending time with her.

Maybe they were more married—more settled—than they thought.

Not that his wife had her mind on the same thing as he.

Amy sighed, clearly still puzzling over what to do about the gift situation, which was definitely different this year.

"Usually, we're not married," he said, picking up the conversation where they'd left off.

Picking out a gift for Amy had always been a challenge. This year, because they now shared the same last name, the stakes were that much higher.

"Afraid of what people will think?" Amy teased.

"Afraid of what *you* will think," he corrected, turning onto his side so he could see her face.

She shifted her gaze from the stars to him. Splaying a

hand across his chest, her touch every bit as soft and gentle as the look in her eyes, she murmured, "I'm not looking to be impressed, Teddy."

"Maybe you should be."

"Why?"

So many reasons. "Because you're my wife."

"And you're my husband. It doesn't mean we have to work overtime trying to buy expensive gifts."

She sure as heck deserved something nice for making him happier than he had ever been in his life. "You're getting something extra nice from me this year. So get used to the idea."

"Which means I have to get you something extra nice."

He shook his head, then leaned over and kissed her forehead, breathing in her sweet lilac scent. "Marrying me was gift enough."

TEDDY, AS IT TURNED OUT, was serious about stargazing, and hoping for snow that clearly was not going to come. Amy soon discovered he also knew his constellations.

"You obviously know your stars, and love doing this," Amy said after a while, sucking on one of the candy canes he'd had in his coat pocket. She savored the sweet taste of peppermint on her tongue. "We've been friends for years. So how come we never did this before now?"

Chuckling, he looked over at her as if he wanted nothing more than to make love to her right then and there. "You're kidding me, right?"

Trying hard not to notice how alluring the day's worth of stubble on his face made him look, Amy hitched in a breath and plastered her most devil-may-care expression on her face. "No. I'm serious."

His eyes held a quiet steadiness that made her tremble. "Because had I done this, with you, like this," he responded softly, "I would have been tempted to jump your bones. And I didn't want to do anything that would jeopardize our friendship."

For a moment, she simply lay there, breathing in the clean male scent of him, trying to decipher what this all meant. "You never...looked at me...that way."

His gaze drifted over her before returning ever so slowly to her face. He made no effort to hide the emotion brimming in his eyes. "Which doesn't mean I didn't notice what a fine, fine woman you are in every respect."

Teddy rolled toward her. He rested his weight on his elbow and propped his head on his upturned hand. He scored his thumb across her lower lip. "I gather from your reaction you never thought about me that way, though."

Amy hedged, not wanting to fib but also not wanting to lead them down a path they had promised themselves they weren't going to go.

"Or did you?" He caressed the curve of her cheek with his fingertip, his face still tantalizingly close to hers.

Amy decided desire was not such a bad thing to admit, particularly when they were trying to have a baby the old-fashioned way. "I might have noticed a thing or two."

Mischief played on his handsome face. "Such as...?"

"You really want to know?" The passion in his voice fueled her own.

He tunneled a hand through her hair. "I really want to know."

"You fill out your jeans nicely." Amy told herself there was nothing dangerous in admitting that.

He regarded her in a manner that was all the more possessive. "So do you, as it happens."

"And I like the muscles in your shoulders and chest and arms."

His hand drifted over her body, eliciting prickles of fire.

The expression in his eyes said he still had his guard up, too. And, like her, he had no intention of taking it all the way down. "You've got some mighty fine curves, too," he told her with an appreciative smile.

Amy drew a deep breath, telling herself they'd be fine as long as they restricted their feelings to the purely physical side of their union.

"But you were off-limits to me in the same way," she continued, somehow managing to keep the unsteadiness inside her out of the timbre of her voice, "so whenever I did notice how well you looked or how good you smelled or how sweet and funny you were, I reminded myself that we were friends and I treasured your friendship." And still do…

"And now?" Teddy lifted her hand to his lips. He kissed her fingertips, the inside of her wrist.

Another waft of desire poured through her, more potent than ever before. "I treasure our marriage. The way everything is starting to work out between us." None of it was exactly the way the romantic side of her had envisioned. Nor did it fall within the parameters of a "normal" marriage. And yet, when she was with Teddy—especially at times like these—she couldn't help but think she'd made the right decision, by deciding to join forces and have a family with him. Deep down, she couldn't help but think they'd find a way to be happy, even if he never cared about her quite the way she cared about him.

"I treasure you," Teddy repeated, rolling so he was on top of her. He framed her face between his rough, callused hands. He studied her, his mouth curving up into a crooked smile. "And now," he continued softly, kissing first one corner of her lips, then the other, "I want us to just be…"

TEDDY HAD BEEN PREPARED to do whatever was necessary to seduce Amy into making love with him beneath the stars. It turned out it wasn't necessary. She looked so full of need for him it nearly stopped his heart.

As he looked into her eyes and lowered his lips to hers, he wanted to tell her she was The One for him.

He wanted to tell her he might even be falling in love with her, but they had promised each other that was a place they wouldn't go. They had promised each other they wouldn't place those kinds of words and expectations on each other. So he tried to show how he felt instead.

Amy kissed him back just as avidly.

She wound her arms around his neck, opened her mouth to the plundering pressure of his, and let her body yield recklessly against his.

Need radiating through him, he tangled his hands in her hair. Her lips were warm and sweet, tasting like peppermint candy. She kissed him with absolutely nothing held back, with a hunger and desperation he not only understood but felt. He kissed her again and again, until whatever reservations she still might be feeling had fled, and she was kissing him back with all the fervor she possessed.

Determined to take his time, to make it last, he unbuttoned her coat, pushed up her sweater and opened her bra. He covered her with his hands, feeling her nipples against his palms. She gasped as his mouth followed the path his hands had blazed. Her nipples budded in his mouth. "Teddy…"

His body throbbed and demanded more. She groaned as his tongue found its way into her mouth once again. The soft surrender of her body pressed against his thrilled him intensely. Knowing she wanted—needed—more, he slipped off her jeans. And thong.

Hardly able to believe they were here like this, that she was his, he looked his fill, studying the rounded fullness of her breasts, the pouting pink nipples, the perfection of her abdomen and sleek, slender thighs. And then his mouth was on her once again. Moving from collarbone to navel to breast, his tempting caresses sent her into a frenzy of wanting that matched his own.

His whole body tightening, he slid ever downward, inhaling the sweet lilac scent of her. He slipped a hand between their bodies. Her hips rose instinctively to meet him as he touched and rubbed and stroked. Finding her as ready as he was for love, he moved upward once again.

Hands under her hips, he lifted her to him.

Amy wasn't sure exactly when Teddy'd had time to take off his coat, open up his fly and push his pants down his thighs. All she knew was that she was naked and he was not, and that in the end it really didn't matter. She wanted him, oh how she wanted him, and judging from the size and heat of him, he had to have her, too.

One hand wrapped around her wrists, anchoring them above her head. His weight pinioned her to the air mattress on the pickup truck bed. Her thighs slid open and she lifted her hips to meet him, thrust for thrust. And then he was kissing her again, showing her exactly how well they fit.

Amy could never remember feeling so complete, so much like a woman, so full of joy. And that was when it began—the fiery need welling up inside her that would not be denied. The realization that something was definitely happening here, beneath the three-quarter moon on this starry Texas night. Something wonderful and completely unprecedented, something solid and real. Something that felt so right, so very much like home.

So it was no surprise when the truck bed grew hot and close, and the warmth of her body gave new heat to his.

Awash in sensation, Amy let her head fall back, her neck arch. Let the abandon overtake her. And then she was moaning, soft and low in her throat, urging him on, letting the last remaining boundaries between them descend into a free-falling ecstasy that warmed her body and filled her soul. And Teddy, bless his heart, was right there with her.

Afterward, they held each other close, cuddling beneath the blanket and the opened-up sleeping bag, the stars an ever-present canopy over their heads.

Teddy stroked a hand down her spine. "Have I told you you're the best Christmas present I ever had?"

Amy snuggled in his arms, loving the way he felt against her, so strong and solid and male.

"I think you just did," she whispered back. "And for the record—" she tilted her head up so she could look into his eyes "—I love having you in my life this way, too."

In fact, I love you, Amy thought tenderly. *Not just as a friend…or a husband. But in that forever kind of way.*

Chapter Twelve

"Are you sure you don't mind meeting me at the chapel?" Teddy asked late the next morning.

Still glowing from the night of lovemaking—both under the stars and in his big comfortable bed—Amy spread tissue paper in two gift boxes, then gently set the pink-and-blue gingham quilts she had made for their niece and nephew on top of it.

"Actually, it's good," Amy said, doing her best to give nothing of her own secret holiday mission away.

Teddy fit the covers on the boxes while she got out the silver wrapping paper. "Because I have a few errands to do, too," Amy continued, aware she was more excited about Christmas than she had been in years. And it was all due to her marriage to Teddy.

Teddy grinned. "And we can't do our errands together."

Hooking his hands around her waist, he pulled her away from the kitchen counter. He fit her lower half against his and placed his lips on the nape of her neck.

She lifted her head to give him better access as he lazily kissed his way across her throat, and into the open vee of her casual blouse. "Because you're off to buy my gift…" she murmured, delighting in his increasingly heated caress.

She jerked in a breath. "Whatever it is." She pulled away just enough so she could look into his eyes and asked with a perfectly straight face, "Sure you don't want to give me a hint?"

He shook his head. "My lips are sealed." He ran the pad of his index finger across her lips, tracing the shape. Her breath soughed out. He took advantage of her willingness to be delayed. Their lips met in a slow, closed-mouth kiss.

Amy grinned, amused at the way he was maintaining his vow of silence. She stood on tiptoe and kissed her way across the column of his throat. "I imagine I could get them open." She ran her hands up and down his back, appreciating the way the strong muscles tensed. Lower still, there was evidence of his immediate arousal.

"I imagine you could." He focused his attention on her earlobe. "However—" his hands came around to claim her breasts "—I was speaking figuratively, not literally."

Amy savored the warm seduction of his touch. "Ah."

It was amazing, how far they had come in just under four weeks. Amazing, how much further she wanted their relationship to grow. And evolve.

"You can have your way with me later." He slid his hands beneath her blouse, beneath the lace of her bra.

Her nipples budded in his palms. Luxuriating in the tenderness of his touch, Amy wrapped her arms around his waist. "Now, that sounds good." She ran her hands down his backside, caressing the taut muscles, cupping him against her.

With a low moan of contentment, he kissed her again, even more possessively. "Have I told you how beautiful you look today?" He sifted his hands through her hair, releasing her reluctantly. He stared down at her in wonderment. "You're absolutely glowing."

Another sign she might be carrying their baby, Amy thought ecstatically, wishing she could take him back to bed and then tell him the news they'd both waited a lifetime to hear.

But wary of getting ahead of herself, of jinxing things in any way, she merely smiled and focused on the important tasks ahead of her. Regretfully, she shooed him toward the door. "You better get going. Our parents will never let you hear the end of it if you're late for the twins' christening."

He reached for his coat. "Not to mention what Rebecca and Trevor would have to say."

Amy smiled. "I'll see you there." She paused to give him another brief kiss.

Teddy hugged her hard. "Drive safe." He turned and headed for the door.

Short minutes later, Amy was on her way, too.

Wary of stopping at the local pharmacy to buy what she needed to find out if the gift she hoped to give her husband for Christmas was indeed possible, Amy went to a neighboring town instead.

Just to be sure, she purchased two different types of home pregnancy testing kits, then headed on back to the Silverado ranch.

The results left her stunned and clearly pinpointed what she had to buy for him. So she picked up the phone and called the store both her sisters frequented, explained the problem and agreed to pay extra for the rush delivery before noon on Christmas Eve.

Only then could she leave for the christening.

By the time she walked into the Laramie Community Chapel, Teddy was waiting for her.

In suit and tie, he looked more handsome than she had ever seen him. He greeted her with a broad smile and a hug.

Minutes later, they stood with their families, watching as Jenny and Joshua were christened.

As she stood there, her hand clasped tightly in Teddy's, Amy couldn't help but think how much her life had changed in the past month. The day after Thanksgiving, when she and Teddy had been touring the storm-damaged building, it had seemed like all her own hopes and dreams had gone up in flames, too.

Slowly, with the help of everyone who treasured the beloved historic landmark, the chapel had been brought back to a state of beauty and grace. Her life had undergone a similar transformation. It was all due to Teddy... and the love she had found for him.

Amy had never known her heart could be so full.

And, predictably, she wasn't the only one who had noticed.

"I've never seen you looking happier," her mother commented after the ceremony, as Amy and the other women gathered in her parents' kitchen to prepare the celebratory buffet dinner.

"I agree," Susie said. She studied the new glow in Amy's cheeks. "In fact," she said, peering even closer, "if I didn't know better, I'd think—"

Amy pressed a fingertip to her sister's lips. "Shhh."

Susie's smile broadened.

Intuitively, Amy could tell her pregnant sister knew.

Rebecca came closer, too. "Is it possible...have you and Teddy fallen head over heels in love with each other?"

Amy knew how *she* felt.

As for Teddy... He certainly looked at her—and

kissed and held her—as if he were feeling the same way. Neither had broached the subject of being in love with each other, because of the promise that they had made to each other when they married. But maybe it was time that changed.

"Let's just say this month has been full of surprises," Amy hedged.

"GOT TO HAND IT TO YOU," Trevor told Teddy, as the three triplets headed out to the woodpile behind Meg and Luke's home to get more firewood for the hearth. Trevor slapped Teddy on the back. "You really pulled off the impossible, making a marriage of convenience work as well as it has. Especially in this day and age."

"What do you mean?" Teddy asked, the gift he'd bought for Amy burning a hole in his pocket.

As much as he had enjoyed seeing Josh and Jenny christened in the chapel...and relished being with family and friends...today he couldn't wait to get out of here and be alone with Amy once again.

"Yep. That's true," Tyler agreed. "People our age aren't inclined to settle for half measures anymore."

Trevor nodded sagely. "They want it all. Love. Passion. Romance."

"In addition to shared values, basic compatibility and the ability to have fun together," Tyler added.

Teddy could tell his brothers were working up to a fishing expedition. Which wasn't surprising. He knew they had been concerned he and Amy were making a big mistake that had the potential to ruin their decades-old friendship. He knew as enamored as they were of their own wives and babies, and baby-on-the-way, that they wanted him—and Amy—to share the same joy. They just hadn't been convinced that he and Amy could make the move from friends to lovers successfully.

And for a time, neither had Teddy.

All that had changed in the past few days and weeks.

Teddy knew he and Amy were right for each other. He knew they were as close to soul mates as any two people were likely to come.

What else could a person want?

Aware his brothers apparently needed some reassurance, Teddy said, "Amy and I have all that."

Tyler and Trevor traded skeptical looks.

"Even love?" Trevor asked.

Tyler held up a hand before Teddy could answer and interjected firmly, "And we're not talking about the kind of love you feel for a lifelong friend, bro. But the real deal."

Teddy's heart filled to capacity as he thought about the only woman who had ever made him feel completely alive.

"But is it true?" Trevor pressed.

Teddy paused, not sure what to say to that. He knew how he felt. He also knew the vow he had made to Amy at the outset. He was a man of his word and could not go back on that promise.

"Amy and I agreed at the outset we would never make that kind of demand on each other," Teddy said with a grimace.

"So you don't love her," Trevor said, still trying to understand.

"At least not the way we love our wives," Tyler ascertained.

Teddy lifted his hands in a careless gesture and saw something flash out of the corner of his eye.

He turned.

Amy was standing there, shivering in the winter air.

It was clear from the look on her face that she had heard every word they had said.

AMY HEARD THE OATH TEDDY muttered. It was enough to burn the rust off a charcoal grill.

"We'll just get this firewood inside." Tyler and Trevor rushed off.

Amy and Teddy faced each other. To her fury, Amy felt her cheeks start to heat up.

"My brothers were just trying to understand our arrangement," Teddy explained awkwardly, approaching her.

So was she.

She stared at him in shock, wondering how she could have been such a fool, how she could not have seen… "So you don't love me." Her voice sounded as cold and defeated as she felt inside.

Teddy looked at her as if he knew this was some kind of a test. One he was determined not to fail.

He shrugged, never looking more like a McCabe male than he did at that moment. Big, strong…implacable.

He took another step closer. Stood, legs braced apart, as if for battle. "I promised you I wouldn't ever bring that kind of…expectation…into our relationship." He grimaced. "I won't."

Which meant, Amy realized sadly, he didn't love her.

Her feelings had changed.

His hadn't.

Yet try as she might, she couldn't bring herself to tell him that, because doing so would be breaking her vow to him.

She had promised him, before they said their vows, that

the friendship they had, and the shared desire for a family, would be enough.

Only to find out, it wasn't, after all.

The really wrenching part, of course, was that she had found everything she had ever dreamed of in her marriage to him. She had found happiness beyond her wildest imaginings, and a love that was strong enough to last a lifetime.

She knew now what all the songs, books and movies were about.

She knew why people in long-term committed relationships were so happy, so at peace.

Teddy didn't because he had yet to experience it.

And that was sadder for Amy than any disappointment she was dealing with.

Because she loved Teddy so much, she wanted him to experience it all, too.

She wanted him to have the kind of love she felt for him.

Even if he didn't feel it for her.

"I think you deserve more than that," she said quietly, knowing—even as her heart was breaking—that this was the biggest sacrifice she had ever made, and the most worthwhile. Because loving someone meant wanting the best for them, even if it wasn't the best for you.

Intuitively seeing the seriousness of the situation, Teddy took her hand and drew her into the playhouse her father had built for them as kids. He shut the door behind them, ensuring a measure of privacy. Although outside the December air was brisk and wintry, inside the six-by-ten wooden structure it felt warm and cozy.

He looked around, found no place for them to sit down or get comfortable, so instead they stood in the center of the playhouse, between the tea table and the shelves filled with toys.

He placed both his hands on her shoulders, as if that would prevent her from running away from what she knew now had been a very huge mistake.

"What are you talking about?" he asked.

Amy forged on in a low, trembling voice. "I know that you think that loving each other—as friends—is going to be enough to get us through a lifelong commitment to each other."

And maybe it would have if she hadn't had a taste of what real love and passion were.

The happiness left his eyes. In its place, something hard and forbidding took over. "I gather you don't agree?" he mused grimly.

Amy's throat ached. "I think we both deserve more."

He stepped back and ran his hands through his hair. "What happened?" he demanded, looking confused. "A few hours ago, we were fine!"

Amy swallowed. "I guess you could say I came to my senses."

He released an impatient breath. "And realized what we have—the passion, the compatibility, the lifelong friendship and the ability to have fun together—is just not good enough."

His sarcasm stung, but it did not change her mind. Her overwhelming need for him to be happy remained intact.

He would not be, if he never experienced love.

Oh, maybe they'd be fine for a while. But then one of two things would happen. He would either realize what had been lacking in his life and regret the way he had sold out, in marrying her. Or he would meet someone else who could give him everything he had ever wanted, and then be torn between what could be and what he had already promised to her.

Either way he would be miserable.

Either way it would be heartbreaking.

And Amy's heart was already crushed enough for both of them.

Resolved to limit the damage as much as she could, Amy offered what little comfort she could, under the circumstances. "Look... We gave it a good try. It just didn't work. That's all."

He stared at her, looking every bit as blindsided by the recent turn of events as she had felt when she walked out into the yard and overheard him talking to his brothers.

"That's not what this is about," he told her angrily.

Eyes burning, she replied warily, "It isn't?"

"No," he snapped. "It's about what your sisters have with my brothers, what Ed and Sheryl have. It's about you wanting a baby so badly you thought you were willing to *settle* for me. Only to find out that you can't live without the kind of deeply romantic connections that they have with their spouses, after all."

"I'm doing this as much for you as for me," Amy cried, hurt he would think she was doing this because she had no regard for his feelings, instead of because she did!

"Bull." He stared at her in mounting disappointment and summed up contemptuously, "If you cared about me and my happiness, you wouldn't be standing here, telling me it's over."

The tears Amy had been holding back began to fall. "Don't you see?" she cried. "It has to be."

"All I see is that what I have to offer isn't enough. It won't ever be enough. You want this marriage to be over?" He took off his wedding ring and pressed it into her fingers. "Consider it ended." Without another glance at her, he stormed out.

Chapter Thirteen

"Working? On Christmas Eve?"

Amy turned to see Trevor and Tyler McCabe standing in the doorway of her greenhouse.

With one sweeping glance, they took in her swollen eyes and red nose, the raft of used tissues sticking out of her pocket. She knew she looked like hell and she could have cared less.

Feeling a lecture she did not want to hear about to commence, she said wryly, "Shouldn't you two be tending to your own wives right now?"

They sauntered in like they owned the place. Trevor spoke first. "Teddy's our triplet. You're our sister-in-law. It's the most important holiday of the year. And you two are not together."

"Therefore," Tyler continued, as they ganged up on either side of her, "this is our problem, too."

No one had to remind her of the sanctity of marriage, Amy thought, which was where this "talk" was going. It was the sacredness of her relationship with Teddy that had forced her out the door, against her will. But, figuring Teddy's brothers didn't need to hear anything Teddy hadn't—and wouldn't—Amy kept silent. Because she knew if Teddy realized she loved him, he would somehow manage to convince her to stay, and she was just selfish enough to want to do it.

Keeping her distance from Teddy, pretending what they'd shared hadn't been enough for her, was the only way she could protect him. And she loved him enough to want to do that. No matter how it hurt her.

Aware Teddy's brothers were still sizing up, trying to figure out how to get through to her, Amy continued planting seeds into snap-apart plastic starter boxes.

Keeping her own ravaged heart under wraps, she forced a cavalier smile that did not reach her eyes. "I beg to differ with you there, cowboys," she said stiffly. "Where—and how—Teddy and I spend the holidays is not your problem."

Accusation glimmered in his hazel eyes, so like Teddy's. "How can you do this to him?" Trevor asked.

"Break his heart that way?" Tyler added.

Amy's hurt erupted. She tossed off her garden gloves and stalked closer. "First of all, saying I damaged his heart would seem to imply that he has feelings for me, other than friendship." She stared them both down. "You both know that's not the case."

Trevor shrugged. "I know what he said."

Tyler shook his head. "I don't believe it."

I wish I didn't, either.

But the answers Teddy had given during the Newlywed Quiz, the fact that all he seemed to want from her was sex and companionship, said otherwise.

"The guy adores you, Amy," Trevor persisted.

"He's never going to be happy without you," Tyler added persuasively.

Amy blinked back tears and went back to planting

seeds. "He will be when he finds someone and falls in love."

Trevor shook his head grimly. "If you think any woman can replace you in his affections, then you really are kidding yourself."

Tyler took up the same drumbeat. "Do you honestly think he would have married anyone else under the same conditions just to have a baby?"

"We've known for years he had a thing for you." Tyler gave Amy a hand with a heavy sack of potting soil.

Trevor picked up a spade and scooped dirt into pots, right alongside Amy. "Teddy just wouldn't admit it to himself."

"Or anyone else," Tyler added.

Amy sighed. What was it about these indefatigable McCabe men? She scowled and propped her hands on her hips. "I'm trying to be noble here, fellas."

Trevor pulled a tissue out of the box on the worktable and handed it to her. "Is that what you call it?"

Amy wiped her running nose and stubbornly maintained her position. "Teddy deserves to have it all."

"Then why," Tyler asked her quietly, "on this—of all days—won't you sacrifice your pride and give it to him?"

TEDDY WAS IN THE STABLE, tending to his horses, when Susie, Rebecca and Jeremy Carrigan walked in. He had an idea why they were here. He did not want to hear it. "Go away."

"Can't," Rebecca said, looking less like a nursing mother and more like the hellion his brother Trevor had chased, tamed and married. "It's Christmas. And we love you even if you are without a doubt the dumbest man on earth."

"Hey," Jeremy interrupted with a frown. "I thought we were going to go easy on him."

Susie scoffed, looking just as untamable as her sister. She told her brother, "That was your plan. Our plan was tough love and kicking butt."

Teddy added supplement to the feed of a pregnant mare and stepped back out of the stall. "I'm sure you three musketeers mean well—"

Susie held up a hand to prevent him from ushering them out. "We want you and Amy back together. Helping your reconciliation along is our Christmas present to her."

Teddy only wished it were that easy.

Not sure when he had ever been this miserable, he shook his head. "It's not going to happen." He looked each Carrigan sibling in the eye. "Amy made it clear to me yesterday that she wants out of this marriage. And since I agreed to let her walk away without a fight if she ever decided that was what she wanted, I have to honor her decision." Even if all he wanted to do was take her in his arms and make love to her again and again, until she understood what it was they had…what he felt.

Susie frowned, the worry back in her eyes. "Splitting up is not what Amy wants."

Teddy moved down the aisle and into the next stall, to give medicine to an ailing foal. "What gives you that idea?"

"Oh, I don't know." Rebecca shrugged. "A little thing like the fact she loves you, perhaps?"

"She never said any such thing," Teddy snapped.

The Carrigan siblings exchanged looks. "Maybe not to you," Susie said finally.

For the first time since he'd left Amy the day before, Teddy felt a flicker of hope. "She told you that she loves me?" he repeated.

"She nearly did yesterday," Rebecca said.

Nearly wasn't the same as *actually*.

"It was in her eyes," Susie protested.

"We were standing in the kitchen at Mom and Dad's, after the christening, and we remarked how happy you both looked," Rebecca continued.

"We asked her if it was possible she had fallen in love with you. She didn't answer us verbally, but it was clear from the look on her face that she was head over heels in love with you. Then she goes off to find you."

Teddy remembered. He would do anything if he could take back that moment in time. But he couldn't. Now the damage was done. "And she overheard me telling my brothers that we weren't in love." She'd looked so crushed, so hurt, it had nearly brought him to his knees.

Jeremy gave Teddy a man-to-man look. "I talked to her this morning. I get the feeling she thinks she is being noble, letting you go."

Noble! What the…? Teddy stepped forward. "I don't want a divorce."

Jeremy lifted a brow. "Then you might want to tell her that before you do something you both regret."

TEDDY SAID GOODBYE TO Amy's siblings and raced inside to shower. He paused only long enough to grab the gift he had purchased for Amy the day before off the top of his dresser and headed out and into the hall. Only to find he was not alone.

Amy was standing in the living room, beside the Christmas tree they had gotten at her ranch and brought back to his. She was dressed in a figure-hugging white cashmere sweater dress. Her honey-blond hair fell in short tousled curls around her face. She was the sweet, sexy personification of his Christmas angel. The woman he wanted to spend the rest of his life with. The lover who had shown him how to open up his heart and give as well as receive. She was here. Now. Tonight.

And she was gazing at him as if she was as unsure of what the future held for them as he was.

"I hope you don't mind." She smiled at him cautiously. "I wanted to add some more decorations."

"I don't mind." Knowing this was his chance, that he damn well better not blow it, Teddy slipped the present in the pocket of his blazer and stepped forward.

It had only been a matter of hours since he had last seen her, held her, kissed her. It felt much longer.

"The truth is, I wanted to talk to you, too." His throat felt tight and his usual easy speech deserted him.

He kept walking until he was close enough to take her hands. "I know I promised you that I would never bring love into our marriage." He took a stabilizing breath. Ignoring the perplexed knit of her eyebrows, he pushed on. "It was a vow I intended to keep. Had you not called me on it yesterday, I might have lived the rest of my life without ever telling you how I really felt and that would have been just plain wrong, because I love you, Amy," he said with all the feeling in his heart. "Not just as a friend," he continued hoarsely as her fingers tightened in his, "although that's certainly part of what I feel for you. But as my wife and the person I want to spend the rest of my days with. So, if you'll forgive me for being a foolish son of a—"

"Oh, Teddy." Amy wrapped her arms around him, hugging him close. Tears spilled down her cheeks. "I love you, too."

She lifted her head. Their lips met in a searing kiss that

sealed the deal and might have gone on forever—or at least until they made their way back to the bedroom—if not for the moisture running down her face.

Tasting salt, he drew back slightly, ending the sweet caress. He ran his thumbs over her cheeks, rubbing away the free-flowing moisture. "Then why are you crying?" he asked her gently.

"Don't worry." She laughed shakily and held up a hand. "It's not PMS."

He chuckled, too. Wondering how she could look so vulnerable and joyous, all at once, he teased back, "I wasn't going to bring that up."

"But it is a hormonal surge."

He paused, not sure what she meant.

Taking him by the hand, she led him toward a corner of the room, where—unobserved by him until now—a ribbon-wrapped, oversize glider-rocker and ottoman sat. He lifted a brow.

"That's part of your Christmas present from me to you. The other part is here." She led him back to their Christmas tree. "Look." She pointed to an ornament on the top branch.

He read the calligraphy inscription. "Baby's First Christmas Rattle." He turned, a question in his eyes, hope in his heart.

"We're expecting. Late next August, if my calculations are correct."

He hugged her to him. They stood there for several moments, holding on to each other, too overcome with emotion to speak. "Talk about a great present," he said at last.

"The best," Amy agreed thickly.

And it was about to get even better. "I've got something

for you, too." Teddy drew back. "Marrying you the way I did, I robbed you of the big wedding, of the joy of having our families present. It's not too late, Amy. Not for the ring." He reached into his pocket and took out the blue velvet box with the diamond solitaire inside. "Not for the ceremony." He took the ring out and slipped it on her finger, next to her wedding band. Like the two of them, it was a perfect fit.

"We've got the community chapel on New Year's Eve. All you have to do is say yes, you'll marry me all over again."

Amy flashed a blissful smile. "I'll marry you. And this time, cowboy, it will be forever."

FOR THE SECOND TIME IN a week, the historic Laramie Community Chapel was filled with holiday greenery and the fragrance of fresh-cut pine—not to mention a collection of Carrigans, McCabes, and many friends.

Amy was wearing an off-the-shoulder satin wedding gown with a tight fitted bodice, full swirling skirt and manageable train. It helped, she thought, having an aunt who made wedding dresses, right there in Laramie. Not to mention enough family to pull everything together for the event in record time.

The evening was everything she had ever dreamed of having. Everything she had ever wanted. Hoped for…

The music started.

Her father held out his arm to her.

"Ready?" he asked.

Her heart full of joy, Amy nodded.

She took his arm and stepped out into the vestibule, watching as Susie and Rebecca proceeded her down the aisle on their husbands' arms.

Then it was her turn.

Eyes locked with Teddy's, she was gliding down the aisle. Receiving her father's kiss as he gave her away. Taking Teddy's hand. Promising to love and to cherish, from this day forward.

Knowing in her heart that this time everything was exactly right.

"I love you," Teddy whispered, just before he kissed her.

"I love you, too," Amy whispered back.

Then their lips met.

Their marriage was official.

Their kiss, oh so real.

A roar of approval filled the sanctuary.

And their future together—the future they had always wanted—began.

* * * * *

Cathy Gillen Thacker's
TEXAS LEGACIES: THE CARRIGANS continues
with THE GENTLEMAN RANCHER,
coming March 2008,
only from Harlequin American Romance!

*Turn the page for a sneak preview
of the first book in the new miniseries*
DIAMONDS DOWN UNDER
from Silhouette Desire®,
VOWS & A VENGEFUL GROOM
by Bronwyn Jameson

*Available January 2008
(SD #1843)*

Silhouette Desire®
Always Powerful, Passionate and Provocative

Kimberley Blackstone didn't notice the waiting horde of media until it was too late. Flashbulbs exploded around her like a New Year's light show. She skidded to a halt, so abruptly her trailing suitcase all but overtook her.

This had to be a case of mistaken identity. Surely. Kimberley hadn't been on the paparazzi hit list for close to a decade, not since she'd estranged herself from her billionaire father and his headline-hungry diamond business.

But, no, it was *her* name they called. *Her* face was the focus of a swarm of lenses that circled her like avid hornets. Her heart started to pound with fear-fueled adrenaline.

What did they want?

What was going on?

With a rising sense of bewilderment she scanned the crowd for a clue, and her gaze fastened on a tall, leonine figure forcing his way to the front. A tall, familiar figure. Her head came up in stunned recognition, and their gazes collided across the sea of heads before the cameras erupted with another barrage of flashes, this time right in her exposed face.

Blinded by the flashbulbs—and by the shock of that

momentary eye-meet—Kimberley didn't realize his intent until he'd forged his way to her side, possibly by the sheer strength of his personality. She felt his arm wrap around her shoulder, pulling her into the protective shelter of his body, allowing her no time to object. No chance to lift her hands to ward him off.

In the space of a hastily drawn breath, she found herself plastered knee-to-nose against six feet two inches of hard-bodied male.

Ric Perrini.

Her lover for ten torrid weeks, her husband for ten tumultuous days.

Her ex for ten tranquil years.

After all this time, he should not have felt so familiar but, oh dear, he did. She knew the scent of that body and its lean, muscular strength. She knew its heat and its slick power and every response it could draw from hers.

She also recognized the ease with which he'd taken control of the moment and the decisiveness of his deep voice when it rumbled close to her ear. "I have a car waiting outside. Is this your only luggage?"

Kimberley nodded. "I assume you will tell me," she said tightly, "what this welcome party is all about."

"Not while the welcome party is within earshot. No."

Barking a request for the cameramen to stand aside, Perrini took her hand and pulled her into step with his ground-eating stride. Kimberley let him, because he was right, damn his arrogant, Italian-suited hide. Despite the speed with which he whisked her across the airport terminal, she could almost feel the hot breath of the pursuing media on her back.

This was neither the time nor the place for explanations. Inside his car, however, she would get answers.

Now that the initial shock had been blown away—by the haste of their retreat, by the heat of her gathering indignation, by the rush of adrenaline fired by Perrini's presence and the looming verbal battle—her brain was starting to tick over. This had to be her father's doing. And if it was a Howard Blackstone publicity ploy, then it had to be about Blackstone Diamonds, the company that ruled his life.

The knowledge made her chest tighten with a familiar ache of disillusionment.

She'd known her father would be flying in from Sydney for today's opening of the newest in his chain of exclusive, high-end jewelry boutiques. The opulent shop front sat adjacent to the rival business where Kimberley worked. No coincidence, she thought bitterly, just as it was no coincidence that Ric Perrini was here in Auckland ushering her to his car.

Perrini was Howard Blackstone's right-hand man, second in command at Blackstone Diamonds, a legacy of his short-lived marriage to the boss's daughter. No doubt her father had sent him to fetch her; the question was *why?*

* * * * *

Get swept away down under with the glitz and glamour of the Blackstone empire as Kimberley tries to determine the real reason behind her "reunion" with Ric....

*Look for VOWS & A VENGEFUL GROOM
by Bronwyn Jameson,
in stores January 2008.*

When Kimberley Blackstone's father is
presumed dead, Kimberley is required to take
over the helm of Blackstone Diamonds. She
has to work closely with her ex, Ric Perrini, to
battle not only the press, but also the fierce
attraction still sizzling between them. Does Ric
feel the same...or is it the power her share of
Blackstone Diamonds will provide him as he
battles for boardroom supremacy.

Look for

VOWS &
A VENGEFUL GROOM

by

BRONWYN
JAMESON

Available January wherever you buy books